The Cost of Atonement

G. S. Carr

The Cost of Atonement

This edition published in 2018

http://www.gscarr.com/

ISBN-13 978-1-73130-991-4

This book is for all the little girls who dreamed they could change the stars. You can do it!

Chapter One

New York City, March 1862

*R*OASTED DUCK. Virginia tensed the moment the delicious aroma reached her nostrils. She slowly opened the door of the cozy brownstone she and her father shared. Eyes searching and ears straining to listen, she attempted to find the source of the problem. Roasted duck with a side of garlic rosemary potatoes and fresh green beans was her favorite meal. Mrs. Josephine, their cook, only made it when she knew something horrible was about to happen and Virginia would need the solace of a comforting meal.

Virginia closed the front door as delicately as possible, pausing every so often when the treacherous hinges squealed in protest. She scanned the narrow hallway leading toward the back of the brownstone. Nothing seemed amiss. Treading lightly, Virginia tiptoed down the hallway toward the parlor so as not to alert anyone to her presence.

There it was—or, more like, there *he* was. Another male corralled by her father, no doubt through an endless litany of lies about how amazing a wife Virginia would make. This man—with his pinched face, beady eyes, and lips so unusually thin they looked like a scowling line drawn on a cartoon character from the local political papers—could be cousins with a naked mole rat.

Deep-set ridges streaked his furrowed forehead. His stony, blank stare carried no emotion. Joy was probably a foreign concept to this man—as well as passion, humor, and anything else necessary to make a marriage enjoyable. More white than brown covered his balding head; he had to be at least fifteen years her senior. Virginia would never agree to marry such a man, even if faced with abject poverty. But, of course, her father didn't care about any of those things. To him, any man willing to remove the burden that was his daughter would make a suitable husband.

As quietly as she'd come, Virginia pedaled backward down the hall, ready to escape to her room. A squeaky floorboard betrayed her retreat, and she looked to the heavens in exasperation. Both men's heads turned in her direction—one with overwhelming cheer, and the other with complete indifference.

"Ah, Virginia, my dearest," her father crooned. "Come, come."

The cheer on her father's face reminded her of a child on Christmas morn. This did not bode well for her. Virginia followed her father's instructions and walked into the sitting room. She stood next to the wing-back chair he occupied with her eyes cast to the ground, refusing to sit, tension coiled in every muscle.

"My dove, you look radiant today, glowing with youth and good health."

Her father had never used such pet names when talking to her. *Thorn in my side. Heathen*, perhaps. Never graceful birds of divine beauty. Of course, the youth and good health portion of his speech was meant for the gentleman in the room, not her. A not-so-subtle way of pointing out that she was still well within her childbearing years.

Virginia was pulled from her angry musings when her father's ragged cough reached her ears. His shoulders shook with the force of it. For a moment, all else was forgotten. His cough had been getting progressively worse as of late; she made a mental note to call the doctor to visit him again soon.

He pulled out a handkerchief to wipe his mouth. *Is that blood?* Virginia squinted at the small piece of white fabric, but her father shoved it into his pocket before she could examine it closely.

"I beg your pardon—the dust lodges in my throat from time to time," her father said, fixing a smile back on his face. He placed a hand in the middle of her back, turning her a bit in the gentleman's direction like a horse breeder showing off his prized mare. Virginia's concern vanished as the anger took hold again.

"Sir Reginald Mumford, may I present to you my daughter, Virginia Lillian Hatcher. Virginia, this is Sir Mumford. He has requested my permission for your hand in marriage, to which I have most ardently agreed."

A deathly silence followed her father's statement. This was the point at which she was expected to preen and smile like a ninny being granted a grandiose favor, but Virginia would do no such thing. *Reginald Mumford.* Even his name sounded as dry as he looked. She had no intention of willingly entering a prison cell in the form of a miserable marriage to this man.

"Darling, where are your manners?" her father asked, pinching the skin beneath her elbow. Virginia barely flinched. "Greet Mr. Mumford properly."

"Mr. Mumford, what a pleasure to make your acquaintance," Virginia said in a dry tone, sarcasm dripping from each syllable.

Either unaware or unaffected by the subtle insult, Reginald tilted his head to several different angles, assessing Virginia. "Not bad. A nice face, but a little on the thin side. However, there is enough meat on her bones to carry several of my sons."

Virginia's mouth slackened, opening and closing as she lost her ability to speak. She knew such chauvinistic men existed, but to be on the receiving end of one's words was a new experience.

Her father's smile spread wider, tinted with a hint of relief. No doubt he'd worried that she had offended Mr. Mumford, ignoring the fact that the gentleman had offended *her*. Mr. Mumford sat blinking, oblivious to the offensiveness of his statements.

"While your assessment of me is not the most unflattering I've heard," Virginia said, "it still did nothing to warm me to the idea of marrying you. How about we learn a little about each other?"

Reginald looked from Virginia to her father, who gave a slight nod of encouragement. "Very well, then. Are you a good seamstress? I find my clothing in need of repair on a rather frequent basis."

Virginia crossed her arms as she stared down her nose at Mr. Mumford. He could have at least pretended to care about who she was as a person. A mischievous smirk spread across Virginia's lips as a thought entered her mind.

"Sewing is a talent I have not perfected, but can manage. Although my heart's passion is being an abolitionist. One day, I want to devote as much of my energy as possible to bringing freedom to all people. After all, we are all human." Virginia stressed the word *human*.

Reginald straightened in his chair, releasing a dismissive scoff. He ignored Virginia's statement and turned to look at her father. "What time frame did you have in mind for the ceremony?"

"I beg your pardon," Virginia fumed, placing her hands on her hips. "I have not agreed to marry you."

Mr. Mumford met Virginia's glare with an unperturbed stare of his own, as if noticing an annoying fly buzzing near his ear. "Madam, I do believe you have the wrong notion about what this is. I only obliged your silly request as a show of goodwill. I need a wife to bear me sons to work on my farm, and I'm not overly choosy about who that woman is. Thus, I have agreed to pay your father a handsome sum of money for you. This is not a matter of the heart. This is business."

"Well, no, I wouldn't phrase it like that," Virginia's father sputtered. A rosy flush crept up his neck and across his face as he sat up straight at the edge of his chair, ready to leap to Mr. Mumford's aid should Virginia decide to wallop him.

"Then how would you phrase it, Father?"

His mouth opened and closed, but the excuses stayed lodged in his throat. At least he had enough of a heart to appear remorseful.

"Never mind—I don't wish to know. Tell Mrs. Josephine her meal smells delicious, and I am sad to miss it. However, my appetite has suddenly abandoned me. I will be in my room if you need me."

Virginia turned to leave the room before either man could reply. As she left, another bout of coughing and the faint whispers of her father's apology reached her ears. But the apology was not meant for her. Virginia swallowed hard, fighting off the quiver of her chin. She hated crying, especially angry, hurt crying.

"No need to apologize," Mr. Mumford replied in a sympathetic voice. "The city has a way of corrupting a parent's good, moral teaching in young women such as Virginia. It gives them crazy notions about independence. Next thing you know, they will be wanting to vote. A few babies and time in the country will fix that."

Virginia didn't wait to hear her father's response. She took the steps two at a time, running up the stairs toward her room as fast as her legs could carry her. Unwelcome tears spilled down her cheeks, adding to her annoyance. She forcefully wiped them away with her fist.

After months of her father trying to pawn her off on another man through marriage, Virginia thought that her heart had been hardened against scenarios such as this. Slamming the door to her room, she threw herself against her bed. Virginia lay on her back, taking deep breaths to calm herself. She continued to wipe away the tears until they finally dried up. Neither her father or any man would ever have the satisfaction of being the reason she cried again.

Chapter Two

THE BRIGHT LIGHT OF the early morning sun filtered through the window above Virginia's writing desk, casting the shadow of her hand over the blank white page of her journal. She normally found solace in her morning journaling, but today the words refused to come.

The pain and disappointment from the events of last night plagued her mind. She needed to put them to paper to free herself of their hold. She placed the tip of her quill to the paper, and again, it froze, unable to find the words to express all the emotions swirling in her heart.

With a growl, Virginia shoved the quill back in its inkwell and slammed the journal shut. She scrubbed her palms over her face, then cradled her head in her hands.

How could life deal her such a hand, and how could she be free of it? A light knock on her bedroom door interrupted her thoughts.

"Enter," Virginia called out, not standing from her writing desk.

The door slowly creaked open. It stood ajar for a moment before her father stuck his graying head around it. His eyes briefly met Virginia's before fluttering away. A slight pink blush covered his neck and ears. Virginia wanted desperately to believe—but dared not hope—that what she saw on her father's face was remorse.

It would be too much to bear if she were to hope he had changed his mind about the marriage and be wrong. Her father shuffled farther into the room until he stood about an arm's length away from Virginia. He was physically close enough to touch, yet emotionally, an ocean of unsaid words stood between them. His eyes darted around the room, landing on the four-poster bed, her porcelain doll, and anything but Virginia's gaze.

The silence stretched between them until it was painful, but Virginia refused to speak first. She gave him her undivided attention, waiting patiently.

He cleared his throat, which led to a slight cough. When it subsided, he said, "Virginia, I do love you. I know that you are of the opinion that my main goal in life is to make you miserable or be rid of you, but it's not. I want you to be happy and well taken care of. I will not live forever, and I want to die knowing that you are secure with a husband. You can learn to love any decent man, if that is what you seek. I will make sure that you have financial security, which is a blessing many want and do not have. But, who will you have to talk to about life in your old age? I beg you: please put your heart aside for a moment and think with your head."

The urge to open her mouth and argue with her father clawed its way through every fiber of her being, demanding release. Mr. Mumford did not strike her as the kind of man who would wish to engage in idle chatter with her either now or in old age. Virginia clamped her mouth shut, gritting her teeth. No matter if she wanted to listen to her father or not, she would be foolish to dismiss his words without thought.

"Thank you for loving me, Father. I will consider your words."

"Good, good," her father said with a relieved sigh. "If your mother could learn to love me, I know any somewhat decent man can win a woman's affections."

A soft smile played across her father's face as his mind slipped into a memory of her mother. It was a rare sight for Virginia, to see him show even this bit of emotion.

"You're not so bad when you try," Virginia replied with a teasing grin.

Her father snorted in return—his way of accepting a compliment. "Mr. Mumford will return in a week. I will not force you to marry him, but please think long and hard about your answer. Also, I plan to place the money he gives me in an account in your name, which you will have immediate access to upon your marriage. I will ask him to sign an antenuptial contract so that all I leave to you upon my death will be yours to control. And even if your future husband is not Mr. Mumford, I will set several thousand dollars of my own money aside for you once you are married so that you can still be your own woman financially."

Virginia's eyebrows rose at that statement. She placed a hand over her rapidly beating heart. So much meaning lay between those words. He was giving her the freedom of choice. Even in marriage, she would have the ability to take care of herself and any resulting children. Her husband would never be able to fully control her. It was the greatest gift her father could give her.

"Thank you." Virginia rose from her chair and wrapped her arms around her father's neck. "I love you. That truly means the world to me."

"Yes, yes," her father replied, patting Virginia's back with stiff, mechanical motions. He allowed the embrace to continue for a few seconds before pulling back and reestablishing the distance between them. The flush on his neck and ears had deepened to a cherry red. "I hope that sentiment lasts after my next announcement."

The smile slipped from Virginia's face, her body going still as she waited for her father to make his announcement.

His eyes again bounced around the room, not meeting hers. "Although I will allow you the choice of marrying Mr. Mumford or not, I do believe you are in need of a companion. Someone to watch out for you and possibly help to soften your...less ladylike edges. I fear I have done a poor job in that respect."

Virginia ran her palms down her skirt, dispelling the rising panic threatening to overtake her. He was giving her a warden, someone to report her every movement back to him. "Someone to make sure I don't run off and join a group of abolitionists before you can sell me to the highest bidder?" she scoffed.

"It is either the companion, or never leaving the house without me."

"And who might this companion be?" Virginia questioned, caution lacing her every word.

"Anna, please come in," her father called out.

Virginia's eyes darted to the bedroom door that still stood ajar. It widened a little more to admit a short cherub of a woman. She bore perfectly pinned, strawberry-blonde curls, pink cheeks that looked as if they'd been dusted with rose petals and stardust, a cute button nose, and a classically stunning, round face. She was so cute Virginia almost forgot she was supposed to be offended by her presence.

"Greetings. You must be Virginia," she chirped before dipping into a low curtsey. "My name is Anna, and it is a pleasure to make your acquaintance. Your father has told me many wonderful things about you. I am happy to be at your service. This job is a blessing; I was down to my last few coins before I contacted your father."

Virginia cursed under her breath. She couldn't turn the woman away after hearing that. Did her father tell Anna to say that? Would it matter if he did? Anna was so adorable Virginia was already having crazy notions about being friends and sharing secrets over tea. Even her voice sounded like the soothing tinkle of delicate bells.

"Pleasure to meet you as well," Virginia replied, holding out her hand.

Anna looked down at the offered hand, then between Virginia and her father, uncertainty shining in her gaze. Women did not shake hands, a fact that Virginia knew but chose to ignore. This wasn't a test necessarily, but it would help shape Virginia's opinion of the other woman.

Virginia's father stood in silence, watching the interaction. No doubt he hoped this situation would end with Virginia accepting her new companion with little to no fuss. Whatever it took to make that a reality, he would allow.

Squaring her shoulders and stiffening her spine, Anna reached out and accepted the offered hand with a smile. The grip was firm; Anna had courage. Virginia liked that. She didn't return the smile, but her eyes softened on the woman before her.

"Well, then, what does a companion do, exactly?" Virginia asked.

Virginia's father deflated, nearly melting into the floor as the worry left his body. The flush left his cheeks, his skin resuming its normal coloring. Maybe he had been less confident about how the meeting would unfold than Virginia had thought. Was she really that stubborn?

"Right, then. I will leave you two ladies to get acquainted." He scuttled out the door before anyone could say another word.

A slight giggle escaped Anna's lips. "He seems relieved. Maybe he thought you were going to eat me alive."

"Possibly. Luckily for you both, I had a filling breakfast," Virginia replied with a deviant smirk. She had to suppress a laugh when the smile slipped from Anna's lips. Good—a healthy amount of fear from the other woman could come in handy. "Well, it looks as if we are stuck together now. I was in the middle of journaling, but I fear my ability to convert my thoughts into the written word has escaped me. I already have plans for the day, though, you may join me if you wish."

Virginia turned and walked out the door, not waiting for a reply. She had accepted that she wouldn't be able to get rid of Anna, but that didn't mean they had to be friends.

Chapter Three

THE WORN-DOWN COLORED man, Mr. Jones, slumped in the chair in front of Charles's desk, had only known a life of trials. No doubt he was a runaway slave, but Charles didn't ask. The weary caution at the edge of his gaze, that constantly darted around the room, told Charles all he needed to know.

"I need that money. What I'm supposed to do when the landlord come knocking wanting his money?" Mr. Jones beseeched Charles in a sullen voice. He twirled his hat in his hands to give his fidgety fingers something to do.

"Don't worry, Mr. Jones. I will do everything in my power to return what was taken from you," Charles said with conviction.

"How?" Mr. Jones barked. Surprise over his outburst shone in his eyes. He clamped his mouth shut, bowing his head. Regaining his composure, he leaned closer to Charles and lowered his voice to say, "Ever since that Dred Scott case, black men don't have the right to sue white men."

"That case refers to federal courts. There are other avenues to retrieve what was taken from you. You provided the labor he required, and he needs to pay you for it. No man, white or black, can get away with such shady business dealings." It burned Charles up inside every time he had to listen to men like Mr. Jones recite stories of being swindled and taken advantage of, with little hope of finding justice. Even worse were the times when there truly was no legal remedy for their case. He had decided to practice law specifically for men like Mr. Jones. To do his part in helping to give them tangible hope for a justice system that worked in their favor.

"We moved into the tenement house two months ago. I can't move my wife and youngins so soon." His shoulders hunched even more as he folded into himself, resting his sharp elbows on his bony knees.

"I will do my best to help," Charles replied with quiet empathy.

"Yeah, that's what all y'all big bug lawyers say. And us colored folk are still out here without a penny to our name." Mr. Jones shoved his hat back on his head as he rose from the chair to exit the office.

Charles watched the man's retreating back with the usual heaviness in his heart that accompanies such meetings.

"It's about time for you to go, isn't it?" Mr. Taylor asked as he walked by. He had been Charles's mentor and the guiding force in his career for the past three years. He also held the unofficial office of ensuring Charles made it to all of his appointments on time.

Charles pulled out his pocket watch to check the time. Sure enough, it was time for him to leave; otherwise, he would be late. In thirty minutes, he would begin his interview for admittance into the New York Bar Association. Charles placed his hand in his left pocket and rubbed the locket he always kept there for luck. He rose from his desk and straightened his cravat and vest. After slipping on his frock coat, he smoothed his hands over his ensemble, then held out his arms and spun for inspection. "How do I look?"

"Like a future lawyer of New York Bar Association," Mr. Taylor said with pride.

"Excellent. If you would have said like a future sailor bound for the docks, I would have been worried."

"Go on, you. Be off and stop delaying." Mr. Taylor kicked the air, booting Charles out of the room.

With a smile at the older man's antics, Charles left the office to begin his commute. Today, he took another step closer to his dreams.

"So, how'd it go?" Andrew inquired.

Charles let the heavy wooden door swing closed behind him, his head hanging low. He ran a hand through his hair, averting his gaze from his friend's. Thomas and Andrew stood before him, eyes wide as they awaited his news.

"Well, come on, then. You're one of the smartest men I know, so it couldn't have been that bad. Tell us," Andrew prodded Charles. His voice held a bit less cheer than his first question, but his smile stayed intact, even if it was a little tighter around the edges.

"Gentlemen," Charles said in a downtrodden tone, eyes glued to the ground.

"Ah, I'm sorry..." Thomas began, but Charles quickly cut him off.

"You are looking at the newest addition to the New York State Bar Association!"

"I knew it! Never doubted it for a second," Andrew cheered.

The wrinkle in his brow and fidgety way he'd shifted from side to side said otherwise, but Charles didn't push the subject. A broad smile swept across his face. Andrew and Thomas pulled him into a collective hug, lifting him off his feet. Hearty pats on the back followed when they placed him back on his feet.

"Of course, you were admitted," Thomas beamed. "You spent months poring over that boring manifesto—*Blackstone's Commentaries*, something or other. You have a law degree from Columbia College School of Law, and you've worked for one of the best law firms in New York City for the past three years. And you have a face that makes the ladies swoon every time you glance their way. If nothing else, those powder-head nobs would have let you in to increase their chances of getting some horizontal refreshment."

Charles and Andrew howled with laughter at Thomas's crude assessment of his merits to be granted the privilege of being a lawyer. Neither Charles nor his friends had any trouble gaining the affections of the opposite sex.

Each man had his own unique charms that bowled the ladies over. Charles with his blond hair, lean, muscular build, and classically beautiful face. Thomas with his mischievous grin that promised any manner of naughty play in store, jet black hair, and crystal blue eyes. And Andrew with his warm honey eyes, large, hard body, and dimple that added a touch of cute to his chiseled jaw and rugged face.

"I agree with most of your assessment. I'm just glad to finally have achieved this dream."

"We have to celebrate," Andrew said with rowdy excitement.

"Of course, we should!" Thomas enthusiastically agreed. "It's about time you released that tight rein on your unyielding self-control to indulge in a few spirits and women."

Charles took a step back, increasing the distance between himself and his friends. He held his hands up in protest. "Alcohol and women addle the brain. Mixing the two together is asking for trouble. Besides," he said, looking Thomas in the eye, "I've seen the women you frequent, and cleanliness is a word they know nothing about."

Thomas laughed harder, unbothered by the comment. "I can't argue with you on that front. One gal smelled so bad, I couldn't even muster the desire to do the deed. I carry a sprig of lavender with me now, just in case." All three men roared with laughter. "But this is a celebration. We will go to the best parlor house in the city. I heard amazing things about the one on Vesey Street. We'll have a good time."

"We'll compromise and indulge in the alcohol, but not the women. I'll even let you pick the establishment," Charles countered. He was by no means a saint, but he wasn't one to share his carnal trysts with others, either. Bedroom doors closed for a reason, after all. Not everyone needed to know what went on behind his.

"Lovely," Andrew replied, slapping his hand on his thigh.

"I can always use a stiff drink. Women, I can take or leave."

"Fine," Thomas grumbled. "But if you aren't rooster-ed up by the end of the night, I'm going to pour beer down your throat until you are!"

Charles and Andrew laughed at their friend, knowing full well that he meant every word he spoke.

"Well, let's get going, then. The sooner the night begins, the sooner it can end," Charles said with a smirk and pat on Thomas's back.

Taking the position of leader of the evening's festivities, Thomas began walking a bit ahead of the other two men, guiding them toward their destination.

Chapter Four

CONNIVING TRICKSTER. THE ESTABLISHMENT Thomas had selected more closely resembled a brothel than a tavern, despite Charles's compromise. Half-dressed women with brightly painted faces and their breasts bared for all to ogle sauntered from table to table, stopping to sit on the laps of the patrons.

Several couples had disappeared up a flight of stairs, returning red-faced and sweaty hours later. An upbeat song filled the room, encouraging the men to shout the words while the pianist made the melody come alive.

Charles had wanted to leave the second they entered, but Thomas grabbed his shoulders, forcing him farther into the seedy establishment. Andrew had been of no assistance; his eyes had locked onto a busty blonde and hadn't left her since they'd walked in.

Thomas's eyes darted around the room, never staying on one woman for too long. He wasn't picky, but a firm believer in the more the merrier when it came to the fairer sex. No doubt the card game Charles insisted they play was the only thing keeping his friends from abandoning him for more lively activities.

"Stare any longer, Andrew, and the woman will have to start charging you for the privilege," Charles said in a sarcastic tone.

"I don't know what you mean," Andrew retorted.

"He means you're so focused on the blonde chit that your poker game is shit and you're sucking the fun out of beating you," Thomas chimed in, a knowing grin pasted on his lips

"You're no better," Andrew countered. "Your eyes have undressed every filly in this room. The only reason you've been able to win a hand is because you're a cheat."

Thomas gasped, placing his hand against his chest in mock offense. "You wound me, sir. No need to tear down my reputation because you were caught with your eyes up a skirt. But, since we are such dear friends, I will pardon your rude accusations."

All three men laughed. Thomas had an astounding gift for the dramatic arts.

Charles shook his head at his rambunctious friends. He placed his cards on the table, then raised his pint in the air. "To friends who make life a bit more colorful."

"To you, for becoming a professional liar and cheat," Andrew added, clinking his glass with Charles's.

"And to you, for your continued health and safety in your foolhardy notion of fighting another man's war," Thomas added, raising his glass as well.

Charles's grip tightened on his glass, lips pausing mid-sip. There were some topics he and his friends did not discuss, the war being the most recent.

"Say what you will, but at least I have the brass to stand up for something I believe in," Andrew countered, voice low with derision. His eyes narrowed on Thomas as he set his glass on the table harder than was necessary.

"And what do you believe in? That the Negro is human and deserves to be free? What if they are? Better them in the fields than us. Besides, what happens when they become free? They'll flood to the north and try to take any factory positions they can get. Then, what? We lose our jobs, our livelihoods. I say if the South wants to keep them, then by all means let them."

Andrew and Charles sat back in their chairs, watching Thomas gulp down his ale after this impassioned speech. Andrew cracked his knuckles, then flexed his fingers as if fighting the urge to wrap his hands around Thomas's neck.

Charles stuck his hand in his left pocket. He ran his fingers over his locket as he rotated his head on his shoulders to release the building tension. Thomas was a dear friend, but statements such as that one made him question the man's heart. He would never know how deeply those words cut Charles.

"Your ignorance is concerning, yet so common I dare say it no longer shocks me," Charles said. "Upsets me, yes—shocks me, no. This war is about so much more than the South being able to keep the blacks and slavery. However, it is still our duty to right this injustice. We whites are not slaves simply by divine coincidence. Who knows, maybe one day they will enslave us." Charles finished his reprimand with a nonchalant shrug.

"Set them free, and we may just find out. Who knows? They may retaliate just to spite us." Back stiff, Thomas glanced between his two friends as if they were the daft ones for not understanding the larger issue underlying the institution of slavery. "And coincidence or not, I could care less. The cards of life have fallen in my favor, and I have no intention of questioning them."

Andrew slammed his fist on the table. Several nearby customers quieted, attention drawn to the storm brewing between the three gentlemen. "You sniveling, sorry excuse for a..."

"Enough." Charles raised his voice to cut through Andrew's heated outburst.

Andrew's eyes flicked to Charles, sharing a look of mutual distaste for the conversation at hand. Grumbling under his breath, he slumped back into his chair, refusing to acknowledge Thomas.

Charles turned his attention to Thomas, appeased that there would be no more outbursts from Andrew. "That statement truly saddens me, dear friend. I hope that one day you will have a change of heart. The last half of this conversation has been anything but delightful, and I truly did not wish to be in this establishment to begin with. I think it is time I took my leave. Thomas, I bid you *adieu*. Are you coming, Andrew?" Charles asked as he pushed his chair back from the table.

Andrew gave a curt nod before rising as well.

Thomas looked at the two men, hands held up in surrender. He even had the audacity to look hurt and confused. "Come on, gents. Is this how we're going to end the evening? We're allowed to have different opinions."

"This is how you decided to end the evening," Andrew sneered. "Next time, it would serve you well to think before you open your mouth. Be lucky I love you like a brother, or you would be laid out on the ground with my fist in your mouth."

Charles picked up his frock coat from the back of his chair and turned to the exit, Andrew on his heels. It was unlikely that Thomas would ever ask for forgiveness, but they would put his comments behind them eventually. Charles knew that he could never change the man's heart, but he wished with all he had that one day his friend's eyes would be opened.

Virginia pointed the rod at the next set of words, written in her delicate loopy hand, on the chalk board of the small, one-room schoolhouse. "Let's begin," she instructed the students.

Women who ranged in age from young to old sat in their chairs, back straight, hands folded on their desks, attention focused on the chalkboard Virginia pointed at.

"Cat, hat, rat, sat," they read aloud in unison.

"Very good," Virginia cheered to the small group. "You all have been such a wonderful group lately; I think I will release you early. Don't forget to practice your spelling and the multiplication problems I assigned. There very well may be a pop quiz during the next lesson."

A collective groan rose from the group. Virginia laughed. They may pretend to loathe the work, but she knew how they really felt. Many of the women, especially the older ones, pored over their work, absorbing everything she presented to them. Some even came up to her after a lesson asking for more books to read. They were voracious learners, and Virginia loved every second she spent helping them achieve their education goals.

"Ms. Hatcher?"

Virginia looked down at Pearl. She was a petite little lady, with glowing onyx skin, no older than about seven years of age. Today, she wore a neatly pressed, brown cotton dress, with her hair neatly braided down. And her shoes, although worn and in need of replacement, were clean. Pearl's mother was a seamstress, and her father worked in one of the factories. They didn't have much, but they always made sure their daughter was well fed and presentable. "How are you today, Pearl?" Virginia asked with the special smile she always had for the little girl.

"I am wonderful today, Ms. Hatcher. Thank you for asking." She held out her hands, which contained a covered dish. "My mama baked a cake last night and wanted me to bring you some."

Virginia took the offered dessert. "Tell your mother I said thank you. I greatly appreciate this."

"I will. Bye, Ms. Hatcher." Parental mission complete, the little girl skipped out of the school room.

The rest of the women filed out of the room, waving and saying their goodbyes. Virginia waved back, a wide smile on her face. Teaching at Mrs. Ruth Washington's School for Colored Women was the highlight of her day. It filled her up with pride and purpose each time she walked through the doors.

"You are a wonderful teacher," Anna said in a voice tinted with reverence. "Did you always want to be a teacher?"

"No. Until about a year ago, I didn't have plans. I assumed I would eventually be married off to the first suitor who would take me. But now, I want to do so much more with my life. In regard to teaching, it found me. I met Mrs. Ruth at the market, and we started chatting. She told me about her school and invited me out for a visit. I fell in love and have been back here, helping out in any way I can, ever since."

"Thank you for bringing me," Anna replied with sincere appreciation.

"Thank you for coming. Come, let us finish returning the room to rights so we can return home."

Anna nodded her head and started picking up books to return to their proper shelves. Virginia glanced at the other woman as she worked. It was nice to share this piece of herself with someone else. *But she is the hired eyes of your father*, she reminded herself. She had to be careful what she allowed her to know and see.

Chapter Five

Black and white. Right and wrong. Good and bad. These ideas floated through Virginia's mind in a web of interconnected, abstract philosophical concepts. Like every day for the past year, they consumed her thoughts. What made one person right and another wrong? What made one person better and another worse? Was it all a matter of perception?

"Oh, do keep up, will you?" Virginia called over her shoulder with an exasperated sigh.

Anna lagged a few feet behind, gulping on air as her stout body waddled along the sidewalk.

Virginia fought the urge to roll her eyes and shake her fist at the sky as she stopped walking to allow the other woman time to catch up. Closing her eyes, she took a deep, calming breath to collect her waning patience. The clomping of horses' hooves followed by the jostling of the carriages they pulled down the worn cobblestone street mixed with the chatter of individuals buying and selling fresh garden fare and other items along the street. The aroma of fresh bread and other baked goods wafted on the cool spring breeze to her nose. Warmth from the midday sun caressed her skin, soothing her.

Opening her eyes, she felt a touch more patience. After all, there was only so much grace you could give when the person annoying you was your warden. But having Anna there was better than the alternative. And Anna wasn't the reason she was upset, she reminded herself. Reading the articles on the various happenings in the abolitionist movement always made her blood boil. It fueled her desire to join the abolitionist movement. To take part in ending the institution that stole her most loved friend and, with her, her heart?

Soleil. The innocent face of her dearest friend, with her sparkling, ocean blue-green eyes and mischievous grin, invaded Virginia's mind before she could stop it. The heavy weight of loss settled on her chest in a crushing vise grip. She lifted her hand to rub away the ache as the bothersome tears that always threatened whenever she thought of her friend stung the backs of her eyes.

It had been almost a year since Virginia had lost the only person in her life with whom she could be her authentic self. She had not laughed until she cried—and had barely laughed at all, for that matter—since Soleil's disappearance.

Kidnapping was a more accurate description of what had happened to Soleil; although, the fine officers of the law in Elba, Alabama, refused to call it such. To do so would mean having to put forth the effort to locate a mulatto woman, a task they refused to do—even if she was the legitimate daughter of a French aristocrat.

"You know, you could slow down a bit. You walk as if you

are constantly in a hurry. Supper is not for another hour, so we do not need to rush home." Anna wheezed the words as she walked toward Virginia. Once she finally caught up, she bent forward in quite an unladylike display, both hands on her hips sucking in air.

"And you, O jailor of mine, could learn to walk faster. Besides, I have matters I want to attend to before supper."

"Like what? Reading the copy of *The Liberation* you purchased when you thought I wasn't looking?"

Virginia narrowed her eyes at the other woman, but refused to affirm or deny her accusation. It took all her strength not to protectively clutch the abolitionist newspaper she had folded within an inch of its life and hidden in her reticule.

Prior to this umpteenth stop in the past quarter mile on their way home, Virginia had allowed her mind to ponder over the paper's contents. This issue, like many before it, advocated for the immediate emancipation of all slaves. It spoke of the humanity of the Negro people and how their captivity was a moral ill against the Creator. Virginia didn't know if she believed in a creator, but she did believe in the humanity of the Negro people.

"Don't worry, I won't tell your father," Anna said on a strained intake of breath. "Look, dear, I know you don't like the fact that your father hired me to keep tabs on you. I barely like it myself. I feel for colored people—I really do—and have no qualms with your interest in the abolitionist movement. But I need the money your father is paying, and thus, you are stuck with me. The least we can do is not make it unbearable for each other. After all, I thought we'd reached a level of understanding at the school. Truce?"

Virginia's lips flattened into a thin white line as she looked down at the small hand Anna extended to her. Tricks and lies were one thing she could not tolerate in anyone. Bringing her hard gaze back to Anna's, she searched the woman's eyes for falsehood. All she could see were peace, a desire for a rest—a long one at that—and possibly a friendship. Resigned to making the best of the situation, Virginia took the offered hand and gave it two strong pumps.

"Good," Anna said with an affirmative nod. "Let us be on our way, then. These pinch-y shoes are tight enough to make the bunions on my big toe howl."

Virginia stifled a grin. Even if begrudgingly, she had to admit that Anna was quite funny. She enjoyed her occasionally odd humor.

With the new truce between them, they continued their journey home. No sooner had they started than the squeal of a high-pitched voice and the rustling of a scuffle reached Virginia's ears. The sounds came from the alley a short distance away. Some people tossed curious glances toward the commotion in the alley as they passed, while others ignored it all together. None entered.

"Help—please!"

The soft, feminine cry spurred Virginia into action. She picked up the skirt of her dress and ran to the alley. A muffled curse escaped her lips at the societal standard of corsets and yards of fabric in women's clothing.

"Wait! Don't you dare go down that alley," Anna shrieked at Virginia's retreating back.

Virginia ignored the words, not pausing long enough to even give the appearance of listening. She soon heard the clacking of Anna's small feet moving at a faster pace than they were probably used to. As she rounded the corner and dashed into the alley, Virginia's blood boiled even hotter at the sight before her.

Three men, each with varying degrees of grime and dirt coating their clothing, surrounded a young colored woman. One of the men was tall, probably twice Virginia's height, and lanky, while the other two were of average build. The young woman wore a simple black dress and white apron, indicative of a normal maid's uniform. Her body, plastered against the brick wall, trembled as her eyes frantically darted from one man to the others.

"Y'all think you can run away from your masters and come up north to steal our jobs and take food from our families' mouths. It ain't right!" the fatter of the two average-height men snarled. "Go back to where you came from."

Virginia watched in horror as the men lifted their fists, ready to swing on the poor girl. Soft whimpers escaped her lips as she curled into herself for protection.

"You, there! Stop this instant," Virginia shouted, dashing up behind the malicious group.

All three men jumped back from their invasion of the woman's space, glancing over their shoulders. As their gazes settled on Virginia, unimpressed and smug sneers replaced the momentary worry that had marred their faces.

"My word." The two huffed words came from right behind Virginia.

She didn't turn to check on Anna, who was probably one wheeze away from a dead faint. She would deal with her—and somehow convince her not to inform her father about this situation—later. Virginia kept her menacing gaze trained on the rascals before her.

"Keep on about your business, little lady. This don't concern you," the tall man said in a tone laced with threat and warning.

"I am not leaving this alley without her." Virginia breathed a mental sigh of relief that she was able to keep her voice from wavering. She even managed to muster a bit of authority in her tone. Facing down three men was not something she'd ever done before, but she refused to back away from helping a woman who needed her.

"How you planning to take the girl from us?"

Virginia reached down and pulled up the hem of her skirt to show a small amount of her petticoat, tapping it twice. She stayed slightly bent over, hovering near the fabric of her skirt. "Hopefully, with no resistance. But if not, then with the revolver I keep strapped to my ankle and never leave home without."

A beat of silence choked the air in the cramped alley as multiple pairs of eyes bounced between the three parties.

"That's right—she'll blow you to your maker!" Anna chimed in, two seconds after the point at which the retort would have been awkward.

Virginia rolled her eyes and sighed. Blundering, gawky quip that it was, at least Anna had yet to back down.

The men shared questioning gazes. Silent questions about the validity of her claim floated between them.

Back straight, hand steady, Virginia stared them down, refusing to be the first to fold.

"Makes me sick, seeing nice ladies like you standing up for them. She don't deserve the breath you wasting to save her," the tall man grumbled as he took a step back. His two companions followed suit, each taking a step away from the young woman who still cowered against the wall. "Dumb Negro wench ain't worth no trouble. Come on, fellas."

Virginia didn't respond. She continued to stand bent with her hand hovering near her skirt, despite the slight burn that had begun creeping through her muscles. Her eyes followed the three men until they disappeared around the corner and out of the alley.

"Well, that was eventful," Anna chimed in, breaking the silence once the men were out of sight.

Virginia smirked at the understatement of those words. Who knew how close they had just come to serious harm? Or worse, death. "Are you all right?" Virginia asked the young woman.

She unfolded her crouched body, clutching the books she carried close to her chest. Her lips spread into a wide smile, making her heart-shaped face even more radiant. Gratitude shone in her vibrant, deep brown eyes. "Yes. Thank you, ma'am! You saved me from what I know would have been a terrible fate. Thank you both," she said, shifting her smile to Anna.

"Just part of my everyday routine. I'm always companion

to the rescue of helpless maidens being harassed by grimy street scum," Anna replied, jovial sarcasm coating her words.

Virginia finally gave in and released a chuckle of joy and relief. Maybe having Anna around wasn't going to be such a burden after all. "Do excuse her. This is more excitement than she has probably had in her entire life. And it was my pleasure to assist you. I would never leave you to suffer at the hands of those pigs. I apologize on their behalf. My name is Virginia," she said, extending her hand to the other woman.

"Again, I thank you from the bottom of my heart. My name is Cora," the woman replied, shifting the books in her arms to accept the offered hand.

Virginia noted the eloquent manner with which Cora spoke, pronouncing each word carefully. Coupled with the three Jane Austen books clutched in her hands, Virginia assumed she was an avid reader—something she had never been. Soleil had teased Virginia to no end about her enmity toward the written word. Even being a teacher hadn't changed that. A pang of sadness coursed through her heart. Pushing the sadness to the back of her mind, Virginia pasted on a smile and focused on Cora.

"You are a brave and unique woman to carry a gun," Cora said.

"I don't," Virginia said with a conspiratorial grin. She lifted the hem of her skirt to show Cora her bare ankle. She then opened her reticule, which held a fan and other knickknacks but no gun. "I'm ecstatic they didn't figure that out."

Cora let out a deep, genuine laugh. The sound flowed through Virginia, soothing a small portion of her bruised heart.

"I'm glad, as well. My gratitude cannot be expressed with words, but I'm afraid I don't have anything to give you in thanks."

Virginia scrunched her face in mock offense. As if she would ever expect payment for being a decent human being. "I expect nothing from you. My best friend in the world was a mulatress. She was taken by slavers about a year ago." Virginia paused, realizing how disjointed her reasoning sounded after the sentences were spoken out loud. She held her hands up, eyes wide, as a light flush crept up her neck. "I'm not saying I saved you because of her—I would have done that anyway. But you matter to me. All people do. I hope I've properly conveyed what I meant."

"Spoken like a true orator," Anna said sarcastically.

Virginia averted her gaze to the brick walls surrounding them, mentally chastising herself for the poor delivery. The eloquent delivery of words had always been Soleil's gift, not hers.

Cora's soft chuckle floated to Virginia's ears, giving her hope that she hadn't completely offended the other woman. When she lifted her eyes, she nearly sighed in relief to see the pleasant smile on Cora's face.

"I understand. Thank you. If I can be so forward, I noticed you have a copy of *The Libertarian* tucked inside your purse." Cora's eyes flitted down to the newspaper that Virginia had forgotten she held under her arm. "If you are ever interested, a group of us meet every Thursday evening to discuss the abolitionist movement and current events in the cause to end slavery. Sometimes, we discuss ways we can help. Usually nothing of major importance, but every little effort helps. We'll be meeting tomorrow at the law office of Mr. William Taylor over on Third and Ninetieth, if you ladies would like to join us."

"I would love to join you," Virginia exclaimed. A wide, almost frenzied grin spread across her lips. "What time should I arrive?"

"Yes, we would be delighted to attend," Anna added. Virginia's gaze darted to her, a sheepish grin on her face. She had forgotten her new companion in her excitement.

Virginia's heart hammered with anticipation. This was it—the thing she hadn't even realized she'd been waiting for. A chance to be a part of something focused on creating equality for all people. She resisted the urge to reach out and pull Cora into a fierce embrace.

"Around six in the evening."

"We'll be there," Virginia said, conviction coloring her words. It would take an act of divine providence to keep her from attending the meeting.

"Wonderful. Well, I must be going. I look forward to seeing you again."

"I, as well." Virginia walked with Cora and Anna the short distance to the alley's entrance in companionable silence.

Chapter Six

"WE HAVE LIMITED RESOURCES, and we have to be wise in how we use them," Mr. Taylor said, meeting the glare of the man standing in front of him. Mr. Taylor had been arguing with the outspoken Mr. Collins for the past twenty minutes.

"Exactly!" Mr. Collins shouted, smacking the back of his right hand into the palm of his left. The color of his face deepened from a strawberry flush to a dark, ruby red. "We finally have a group of men, free and slave, willing to revolt against the Boyd Plantation. That would free over forty slaves and cripple that town financially. What could be a wiser use of our resources than sending rifles down to them?"

Charles sat in his chair near the large bay windows and front door of the small room in the law office, watching the two men verbally spar. The blinds had been drawn closed to give privacy to the room's occupants. The four desks that normally occupied the center of the room in two neat rows had been pushed against the walls to make space for the lecture-style chair arrangement.

Mr. Taylor stood at a small podium set before the audience, a little to the left of the door that led into his office. No decorations adorned the bare wooden walls, as Mr. Taylor was not a man who would purchase such frivolous things.

Mr. Taylor had been hosting this gathering of men interested in helping the fight to abolish slavery during the three years Charles had been apprenticing in his office. They were the highlight of his week. Mr. Taylor had offered him a permanent position in his practice, which Charles had gladly accepted. Mr. Taylor was one of the best lawyers in New York City involved in the fight for freedom of all men. There was much he still had to learn from him.

This week's meeting had drawn a larger crowd of people than usual, all of whom sat at the edge of their seats, riveted by the argument taking place. All twenty chairs were occupied, with a few individuals standing along the wall. Men—black and white—sat and stood side by side, weighing the words of the two men in front of them.

Mr. Collins stood waiting for Mr. Taylor to finish his rebuttal.

"I understand, George, but you know I don't condone violence. We can extract those people without the need for bloodshed. There is..."

Charles's attention was drawn to the front door that slowly creaked open. All sound suddenly ceased as a young woman walked in. *It's her!* Charles watched the beautiful redhead slip into the room, standing off to the back so as not to disrupt the meeting.

He had seen that stunning face once before, a little less

than a year ago. She still looked as radiant as he remembered, if not more so. Her emerald green eyes, alight with passion, locked onto the lively discussion at the front of the room. She clasped her gloved hands together in front of her, thumbs flicking each other. The slightest sound sent her gaze to the door, as if she was waiting for a monster to walk through and eat her. Either that, or an angry guardian who had forbidden her to come.

The corners of Charles's mouth rose into a pleased grin. She was a rebellious spirit; he had seen it a year ago as they danced the night away. He had not expected to ever see her again, but was not disappointed that he had. Charles rose from his chair, placed his frock coat over it so that no one would take it, and strode over to the new guest. "Today is a wonderful day, indeed," Charles whispered near the young woman's ear.

She jumped, a soft, muffled yelp escaping her lips. Heated eyes rounded on Charles, ready, no doubt, to give him the worst tongue-lashing he'd received in a long time. But all the righteous indignation vanished as her eyes widened from their previously venomous glare. "You!" she exclaimed on a whisper.

So she remembered him as well. Her mouth hung open; her head shaking side to side as if she was seeing something that could not possibly be real. But he was real, and he was not letting her leave tonight without talking to him. "It's wonderful to see you again as well, Virginia. Too bad you left me so abruptly that night. If you hadn't, who knows how many times we could have been graced with each other's presence over the past year."

Disbelief melted into amusement, her bright eyes alight with mirth. Her right eyebrow rose as her lips pursed. "You remember my name."

It was a statement, but Charles answered it anyway. "I do."

"Well, sir," she replied, emphasizing the word *sir*, "I don't know what you think happened between us, but I assure you our acquaintance was not destined to move past that evening." Virginia raised an eyebrow driving her point home. "Before I forget, if you would be willing to make yourself useful, please, tell me if Cora is in attendance."

"She's not," Charles replied with an amused smirk at her underhanded barb. "I think her employer needed her to work a dinner party this evening."

"Shame. I was looking forward to seeing her again. Thank you for that information. Now, please, stop being so rude by talking while others are speaking. I actually came here to learn and listen." Virginia turned so that her back faced Charles, officially blocking him out.

Several sets of eyes from neighboring attendees turned in their direction; most wore pinched expressions. Lips pressed into thin white slashes as their heads shook with disapproval. Some even cleared their throats to further drive their point home.

Charles didn't care. This was the woman who had haunted his dreams for several months after the night they had met. Wonderful dreams. He wasn't about to give up the opportunity to talk with her. Another chance such as this may never present itself again. "I am not leaving here tonight without having a proper conversation with you. This is your first and only warning."

Virginia did not answer him. A small smile playing across her lips served as Charles's only indicator that she had even heard him. Charles pushed off the wall and strolled back to his chair, the conversation far from over.

Chapter Seven

VIRGINIA FOCUSED ON KEEPING her breathing even and steady, despite the hammering of her heart in her chest. The erratic rhythm made each breath a near impossible task. *What is he doing here?* Against her wishes, her eyes gradually drifted to Charles. He lounged back in his chair, right leg resting on his left knee, hands clasped over the right knee. A light smattering of blond stubble covered his strong, square jaw. His luminous, turquoise eyes focused on the two men who loudly debated some topic Virginia had missed.

Charles was... Virginia scoured her brain for the right words. Elegant, alluring, enticing, handsome. He was the only man to ever steal her breath away and make her wish that she was a little more refined. That she was a touch more a proper lady so that she could be worthy of such a gentleman. But even if she was those things, she was not the same woman he had met a year ago.

Virginia fidgeted with the skirt of her dress, running her hands over the material several times to smooth out the nonexistent wrinkles. Charles abruptly turned his head in Virginia's direction, catching her in the act of staring. She averted her gaze to the floor, heat rising up her neck at being caught.

Why was she even watching him in the first place? Distractions in the form of handsome men with dazzling smiles were no longer a luxury she would allow herself. Her priorities were different now, greater than herself. Greater than Charles.

Virginia turned her attention back to the men at the front of the room. The one named Mr. Collins, she believed, sat down after he'd finally finished beating Mr. Taylor over the head with his point.

"Thank you, Mr. Collins, for expressing your concerns. They have been documented and will be considered." Mr. Taylor was obviously a very diplomatic man. Not once did he give in to the impulse to shout over Mr. Collins, despite the countless times the other man had done the same. "The floor is now open again. Does anyone else have an issue they would like to address?"

A tall, well-muscled, burly man, who reminded Virginia of a mountain, stood up. His suit was tailored to fit his large frame. Sharp cufflinks adorned his shirt, and a large gold ring encrusted with matching jewels and intricate engraving rested on his left index finger. He twirled the ring as he opened his mouth to speak. "Good evening," he began.

Virginia noted the British lilt in his voice.

"My name is Richard. I come before you today in need of assistance. There is a colored woman in Tennessee that I need to rescue. She is being held by a vicious man, from whom I tried to purchase her, but my request was denied. Thus, I now seek other ways in which to set her free."

"You mean she is a slave," Mr. Collins chimed in.

Virginia groaned under her breath. *Not this opinionated boor again.*

"Yes, sir, she is," Richard replied, turning to face him.

Mr. Collins sat up in his chair, his full attention on Richard. His head tilted to the side as he searched the younger man's eyes, though, for what, Virginia didn't know. Richard didn't flinch under the other man's scrutiny. He waited, hands clasped behind his back.

Mr. Collins straightened and leaned back in his chair. "Very well, then. Tell us more."

"I can fund the entire journey. I only need someone to connect me with the right people to help me bring her to freedom."

"You mean you want to be put in contact with those on the Underground Railroad so that you can steal her away from her master," Mr. Collins interjected again. Subtlety was not this man's specialty. Virginia admired that, even if it could be a bit annoying.

"Yes, sir. That is exactly my plan," Richard confirmed.

"Why? Why this particular woman?"

Richard shifted on his feet, looking away from Mr. Collins. He rubbed his hands down his pant legs, eyes trained on the floor. "My reasons are my own, sir. I only need to know if I will find assistance here or not."

Mr. Collins raised an eyebrow at the younger man's response. The corner of his lip kicked up in a grin. Something about Richard's response had caught his attention, though, what exactly that was, Virginia didn't know.

"Right, then," Mr. Taylor spoke up, breaking through the tension between the two men. "Since your situation is a personal matter, we will discuss it in more detail after the meeting. We would like to keep the meeting time designated for matters that affect a large portion of the group or the community as a whole."

"Thank you, sir," Richard replied, taking his seat again.

"Of course, young man. Anyone else have anything they would like to discuss?"

Several hands shot into the air. Mr. Taylor selected a new person, who stood and began their speech to the group. Virginia didn't hear a word they said. Instead, her attention was consumed by the large British man with sad eyes. Why was he attempting to free a colored woman? What was he to gain by doing so?

Virginia's gaze flicked over to Charles. She hated to ask, but maybe he could see something in this situation that she clearly couldn't. She tiptoed over to his chair and leaned close to his ear. "Why does he want to save that woman?"

"Because he loves her, of course."

Virginia straightened, mouth hanging open. Visions of the past slammed into her, nearly knocking her off her feet. The face of a brown angel with stars in her eyes every time she looked at a certain young man came to Virginia's mind. Soleil had loved Alex with everything in her, and that love had been stolen from her.

It had nearly broken Alex the night Soleil was taken. And

here stood another man in love with a woman society deemed to be the wrong color. But Virginia knew that the heart beats the same red blood through the veins of white and black men alike. She had to help him. She had to play some part in helping this man reclaim his love.

"Thought you could leave me behind, did you?"

Virginia turned to face Anna's pinched face.

The tiny woman's hands were fisted on her hips; her nostrils flared as she glared up at Virginia.

"Hello, Anna," Virginia whispered in an overly cheery voice. "There are some activities a woman would like to partake in on her own."

"You know why..."

"Shhh." Virginia cut her off. "Don't be rude. The meeting is still underway. We can talk later."

Anna narrowed her eyes at Virginia but remained quiet. Virginia turned back to the men, but her attention was far from focused on what they were saying. She didn't have any personal qualms with Anna, but she wanted to experience this evening by herself. She'd purposely left early without telling Anna in hopes that the other woman wouldn't follow. But, no matter what, she wouldn't allow her enjoyment of the evening to be tainted.

Chapter Eight

FTER ANOTHER THIRTY OR so minutes of people stating their concerns or making suggestions to the group, Mr. Taylor called the meeting to a close. Some guests rose to leave, while others stayed and chatted amongst themselves. Mr. Taylor and Mr. Collins gathered around Richard, continuing their conversation.

Virginia strolled closer to the small group of men to listen in on their conversation. She stood near the wall, back to the men, pretending to look at a plaque hanging there.

"Please, young man, tell us a little more about your situation," Mr. Taylor said in a comforting tone.

Richard took a deep breath before speaking. "Gentlemen, I hope I can make my next statement without fear of retaliation on your part."

"Of course," Mr. Collins stated with reassuring certainty. "We do not believe that slavery needs to be abolished only on some moral ground. We believe it because we know that all men are equal and have the right to be treated as such. Whatever you say to us will be kept in the strictest confidence."

"The young woman I mentioned earlier is named Rose Fletcher. She is the love of my life. I met her at the market one day, and she took my breath away the moment I saw her. I care nothing about the law of man, because only God's law matters. I married her before God about seven months ago. We have kept our relationship a secret until now, but the time has come for me to rescue her. I want to take her back to England with me. There she can live as my wife deserves."

Virginia placed her hand over her heart, wanting to swoon over his words. How he reminded her of Alex. Forgetting that she was supposed to be pretending not to listen, she turned her head, eyes glazed with tears, toward the small group of men.

"What are you doing?"

Virginia jumped, startled by the male voice so close to her. She whipped her head back around to come face to face with Charles. The tops of her ears and her cheeks heated at being caught. Not willing to show her embarrassment, Virginia straightened her back and lifted her head high in superiority. "Not being so rude as to sneak up on others, that's for certain."

"Ah, only rude enough to listen in on the conversation of others."

Virginia gasped, as a proper lady should in such a situation. "How dare you accuse me of such a thing."

"How dare you do such a thing," Charles retorted with a mocking grin.

Fending outrage, Virginia harrumphed, then turned on her heels to walk toward the front door. It was well past her curfew, and she needed to be heading home anyway. It was a risk being out as long as she had.

She searched the room and found Anna talking with another woman. They chatted animatedly, leaning close like old friends sharing a long-overdue gossip session. Coming close but not interrupting, Virginia waved her hand to get Anna's attention. It took several tries, as Anna was engrossed in her conversation with the other woman, but eventually, she noticed Virginia and excused herself from her conversation.

"Well, this was a lovely evening," Anna beamed as she walked up to Virginia.

"Yes, I agree. It was." Virginia held the door open for Anna to walk through. The chill of the spring evening enveloped them as they stepped onto the street, causing Virginia to pull her shawl a little tighter around her shoulders.

"And that young man coming here to ask for assistance to free his woman, that was a gutsy request. Yes, these are abolitionists, but not everyone agrees with the mixing of the races. He was very brave."

"And do you?"

"Do I, what?"

"Agree with the mixing of the races," Virginia asked, her pointed gaze trained on Anna. The question was not a test. She would not hate Anna because of her answer, but it was important.

"We are all people. Same blood and bones," Anna said matter-of-factly. "The heart loves who the heart loves, and I have no problems with that."

Virginia smiled at Anna. She was beginning to like her more and more. Maybe her father's plan wasn't as much of a burden as she originally thought. Proving herself to be even more of an asset, Anna stuck out her hand to wave down a passing hack. The driver pulled to a stop in front of them and stepped down to open the door. Virginia and Anna allowed him their hands to help them into the carriage's interior, then settled into their seats.

What would Charles's answer be to that question? With that thought, his handsome face and mischievous grin invaded her mind. Virginia smiled to herself, remembering having that grin trained on her. He was a handsome devil. There was probably a long list of broken-hearted ladies who'd fallen victim to that grin, which was all the more reason to keep her distance. Besides, she had goals in life that a husband would only prove a hindrance to accomplishing.

Virginia settled further into the soft interior of the small carriage, willing her mind to abandon thoughts of Charles. If only it would listen to her request.

Virginia sat at her writing desk, scribbling furiously across the page of her journal. The writer's block which had plagued her yesterday had vanished. Inspired by her newest muse, the young man named Richard, she poured words on the page of her journal so quickly her hand had trouble keeping pace with her mind.

My heart swelled with joy, sadness, and hope hearing his conviction as he spoke of his desire to rescue his woman. I have not seen nor spoken with Alex since the day of Soleil's disappearance, but hearing Richard speak made me hurt for him and the distance between us. It is as if I lost two dear friends that day.

Alex is a man with his own demons to battle, and I do not blame him for what happened to Soleil, but his inability to stand up to his father and profess his love for Soleil vexed me to no end. It was so refreshing to hear Richard claim his love for a colored woman in front of a room of strangers! The bravery and strength he exhibited shocked me to nearly a dead faint. I truly do hope he can find his way back to his woman and she obtains the freedom she rightfully deserves. Many blessings and...

Virginia's pen halted its movement as a light knock sounded on the door. Placing the quill beside her journal, she rose to answer. Swinging the door wide, she was greeted by Anna and the widest smile a human face could produce. Anna's eyes were stretched wide open, nearly bulging from her head. Her smile was so large it caused the muscles in her neck to jut from her skin and gave a view of all the teeth in her small mouth. She fidgeted in place, unable to stay still.

"I would ask if you are excited about something, but I feel that would be a needless query. Is the excitement something I should be sharing in?"

"Yes! You have a visitor. A nice one. A lovely one. One that you will be more than happy to receive. One that..."

"Yes, yes, I understand. Do not combust into flames of moronic female enthusiasm. No visitor could be that important."

"This one might be! I will let him know you are on your way," Anna nearly sang before she bounced off toward the stairs.

Did she say 'him'? Virginia pondered who the visitor could

be. Her list of male acquaintances was...well, zero. Especially any that would visit in the early afternoon. Mr. Mumford was not due for his return visit for several days, although, his need for a breeding wife could have escalated. Perhaps he realized that he was near the age classified as ancient, and his ability to perform his part in making a child was diminishing.

Virginia walked back to her desk, shook the sander over her journal, wiped away the excess, then closed and placed it in the drawer. She put on her slippers and left her room to meet her guest.

Chapter Nine

VIRGINIA'S HEART BEGAN HAMMERING in her chest the moment she walked into the sitting room. A chill ran up her spine, and pulling breath into her lungs became increasingly more difficult.

Charles stood in front of the bookshelf, perusing the titles. The bright light from the window shone on his back, setting his golden mane ablaze.

Virginia stood in the doorway, unable to make her feet carry her into the room. Her mouth parted slightly as she gawked at the handsome male specimen. With his back to her, Virginia could look her fill without fear of being caught.

As her eyes roamed his well-muscled form, the fog of desire slowly ebbed to make room for more rational thought. Virginia's brows furrowed in confusion. What was he doing in her sitting room? More importantly, how did he know where she lived? Did he follow her home? How long would it take for the police to make it to her home?

Virginia made a mental note to investigate the answer to that last question in the near future. *Better to know than to wonder and die a horrible death.*

Gathering her composure, Virginia cleared her throat and crossed the threshold into the room. "This is a surprise; although, I am unsure if I should consider it pleasant or not."

Before Charles could answer, a beaming Anna skipped into the room with a tray of tea and cakes. Virginia so rarely entertained guests these days it had slipped her mind to send for the tea.

"Thank you, Anna. My manners would suffer without you," Virginia said with a pleasant smile.

"My pleasure."

"Please, set the tray down, and I will pour."

Anna placed the tray on the table between the wing-back chair and the sofa, then shuffled to a small wooden chair in the corner of the room. She picked up the needlework she must have placed there at some point and pretended to concentrate on it; although, Virginia knew she was still listening.

Such was life with a chaperone disguised as a companion. No conversation would ever be private again.

"Please, sir, take a seat, and I will pour us some tea," Virginia said to Charles, gesturing toward the sofa. She took a seat in the wing-back and poured the tea. Once Charles was settled, she handed him a cup, then pierced him with her steely gaze. "Now, back to the nature of your intrusion. What do you want, and how did you obtain my address? Please, be advised that this tea is very hot, and if your answer is not to my liking, some may find its way into your lap. Accidentally, of course."

"Of course," Charles said, amusement lacing his words. He took a slow, deliberate sip of his tea, eyes locked on Virginia.

Charles crossed his ankle over his knee and picked a few errant specks of dust from his jacket before he spoke. "To answer your question, I did not follow you home, if that is what you think. I was invited here today."

"Invited? By whom?"

"By the lovely Ms. Anna. By the way, this is a wonderful brew. I do thank you," Charles said, raising the cup to Anna in salute.

"You're most welcome," Anna preened from the corner.

That traitor! Yes, her eyes had wandered to Charles multiple times over the previous evening, and yes, she had looked with more than a little appreciation. But that did not give Anna the right to invite him over for tea. Virginia shot a murderous glare at the petite woman cowering behind her needlework. She would have to talk with Anna about the boundaries of their relationship.

"If you hold that cup any tighter, I'm afraid you will break it," Charles quipped.

A small gasp escaped Virginia's lips as she glanced down at her tea cup. Indeed, her hands strangled the cup as if it had committed a severe grievance against her. She loosened her grip, a light flush creeping up across her cheeks.

"You can't be mad at Anna. It took quite a bit of begging on my part to pry the information from her. I practically had to promise her my first born to be granted this opportunity to see you again."

Virginia perked up, sitting straighter in her chair. He had begged to know more information about her? Not that it made a difference to her, of course. "I am unsure if I should label that bit of information as romantic or psychotic."

"Maybe a bit of both."

Virginia fought a grin. Why did he have to be handsome *and* witty? "Well, sir, you have seen me again. Now what do you plan to do?"

"You like to get straight to the point. A quality I admire," Charles said as he placed his cup of tea back on the tray. "I've come to invite you for a walk through Central Park."

"I could use a bit of exercise," Virginia said slowly as if she were taking the time to think over her answer. In reality, she wanted to say yes as soon as he asked. "Let me retrieve my shawl, and I will be right down."

"Yes, I shall get mine as well," Anna chimed in.

Virginia glanced at the other woman, annoyance simmering in the depths of her eyes. She knew she couldn't argue with Anna about coming. After all, the majority of the job her father paid Anna for centered around watching every move she made. But Virginia wished, this once, she would heed the fact that she wasn't wanted and feign illness or any other means of staying home. Alas, her wishes were not meant to come true. Anna merrily skipped from the room to prepare for their outing.

"I shall return shortly," Virginia said to Charles with a strained smile.

"And I shall await your return."

The cool spring breeze penetrated the layers of cotton

fabric of Virginia's dress, caressing the skin of her arms and legs, leaving a trail of goose flesh along its path. Despite the cooler temperature, a contented warmth blazed inside Virginia. She walked arm and arm with Charles at a leisurely pace along a well-worn path through the park. Other couples milled about, engaged in their own conversations. And to her credit, Anna stayed several feet back giving them a sense of privacy.

Charles had proven himself to be an exceptional conversationalist. Virginia laughed more in the short time they'd spent together than she had in the past several months.

"Surely, you jest, sir. Why would you even want to train a pig to ride?"

"I was a mischievous youth. It was something to do to keep myself entertained. They were slippery suckers, and it provided a challenge. My parents hated it. Each day, my stench grew worse than the last, until my mother finally became tired of it and newly scrubbed the skin from my body in a boiling hot bath. After that, I retired my title as the family pig rider."

Virginia laughed until her cheeks hurt, imagining a young Charles galloping around on a pig as if it were a horse. "Can you blame her? I would have done the same."

"Yes, well, what mischievous behavior did you get into in your youth?"

"Anything and everything. My mother died when I was still in my tenth year. My father raised me and allowed me to raise havoc as I pleased. I can beat nearly anyone in a horse race, and loathe riding side saddle. I can shoot a bow and arrow like the best Indian warrior. And in my more deviant days, I learned the art of pick-pocketing."

"The art, you say," Charles said, raising an eyebrow at Virginia's statement.

"Yes!" Virginia exclaimed with a firm nod, defending her statement. "It takes great skill to lift someone's belongings off their person without them noticing."

"And why would you want to learn this art?"

"As you said, it was something to keep myself entertained." Virginia gave a nonchalant shrug. "By the way, you seemed to have dropped this." Virginia lifted her hand, which held Charles's billfold. Her face was every bit the innocent young lady, helping return a gentleman's belongings, she pretended to be.

His eyes widened before he erupted into laughter. "Impressive. Now, never do that again, my little swindler," Charles said as he plucked the billfold from Virginia's hands. "What other tricks do you know?"

"Maybe, one day, you'll be lucky enough to see," she said saucily.

Virginia's smile widened. She was openly flirting with him, and she liked it. She was rather good at it. Granted, nothing would come of it. Virginia had plans for her life that didn't include a man. But, for now, it was fun nonetheless.

Chapter Ten

VIRGINIA CHECKED HER HAIR in the mirror, turning her head from side to side, making sure not a single strand was out of place. Satisfied, she pinched her cheeks several times to give them a rosy coloring before leaving her bedroom.

Like every day for the past three days, Anna had come to inform her that Charles waited for her in the parlor. His unannounced visits had become a sort of game for them. One that she had come to look forward to, even if she would never admit it out loud. He'd come by and pick her up and take her on little adventures. Yesterday, he'd taken her bowling, which was a new and thrilling experience.

Walking into the parlor, she found Charles perched in his usual spot on the couch reading a dime novel. He'd taken to sitting closer to the middle as of late, so when she sat beside him they either touched or brushed against each other.

"Good afternoon to you, my uninvited guest," Virginia said with feigned censure. Charles looked up, a breathtaking smile on his full lips.

"Good afternoon to you, my delicate flower, who enjoys my visits despite her complaints."

Virginia couldn't fight the smile that spread over her lips at his reply. Yes, she enjoyed the visits, and even his pet names, but she would not stop her complaining any time soon. If for no other reason, she enjoyed the playful banter too much. "So what activity do you have planned for us today?"

"Today, I..."

Charles's reply was cut short when Virginia's father marched into the parlor, his face a deep, pomegranate red. He moved like a raging storm, arms stiff at his sides, shoulders bunched toward his neck. "Virginia, you shall never believe what..."

Finally seeing Charles, he snapped his mouth shut and came to an abrupt halt. A large, almost manic smile spread across his face, the rant from mere seconds ago already forgotten. His coloring slowly resumed its peachy complexion. "I beg your pardon—I did not know Virginia was entertaining a guest. My name is Robert. How do you do?" her father said, extending his hand to Charles, who stood to shake it.

"It is a pleasure to make your acquaintance. I am Charles Willcox, Esquire."

Hearing that last bit of news, Robert performed the impossible feat of making his smile spread wider. His eyes lit with excitement and opportunity. "You are the young man that has been visiting my daughter as of late. A lawyer?! Are you wed?"

"Father!" Virginia shouted, rising to her feet like a furious siren, her face taking on a red hue equal to her father's previous one.

"Calm down, girl. That is a legitimate question I can ask a man who has come to call on my daughter."

"It is rude and improper!" Virginia fumed. She crossed her arms over her chest and dropped back down into her chair with a huff.

"Since when does propriety hold sway over you?" Robert gave a dismissive snort, as if hearing his daughter chastising him about social protocol was the most ludicrous thing he'd ever heard. He opened his mouth to speak further, but a ragged cough sprang forth instead.

Virginia came to his side and rubbed his back, her anger melting into concern.

He pulled out his handkerchief to cover his mouth as he shooed Virginia's hand. "I'm all right. No need to worry."

But worrying was exactly what Virginia did; his cough had been more frequent and rougher as of late.

Robert stepped out of Virginia's reach, focusing his attention on Charles. "Pardon me. The dust hasn't been agreeing with me lately, but nothing to fret about. More importantly, I must ask: have I seen you before? I feel that I have."

"I attended the birthday celebration of Soleil Dufor this past spring. That is where I had the pleasure of meeting your daughter."

"Dreadful thing that happened to the poor girl," Robert said with a gloomy sigh. He had genuinely cared for Soleil, Virginia knew. Never had he ever spoken a word against her or tried to hinder the friendship between the two young women.

"I couldn't agree more, which is why I want to dedicate my career to helping all persons of color, Negro and Native, find lasting freedom and peace."

"Good for you. We need more young men like you." Robert gave Charles an encouraging pat on the back. "Let us sit. Virginia, would you please pour another cup?"

"Of course, Father."

They all took their seats, and Virginia did as her father asked and poured a cup for him. She added a touch of honey to her father's to help soothe his cough.

Robert took a sip, savoring the warm liquid coating his throat as he swallowed. "So, if it has been nearly a year since you met my daughter, how is it that you are coming around to visit now?"

Charles chuckled at the older man's blunt question.

Virginia wanted to be embarrassed, but he was her father and she expected nothing less from him.

"By chance, luck, or divine providence, I had the pleasure of being reacquainted with Virginia three days ago. My original plan was to wait a few days before visiting to allow her time to fret over me"—Charles winked at Virginia, a sly grin on his lips—"but I couldn't wait. I've spent time with Virginia every day since our reunion. Although, today, I came to tell her farewell, but only for a short while. I will now be accompanying a friend to Tennessee to retrieve his lady love, and we leave at first light."

Virginia sat erect, her curiosity piqued. A swarm of fluttering began in her stomach. She leaned forward, sliding to the edge of her seat. "The young man from that night? Richard?"

"Yes, the very one." Charles raised an eyebrow, curiosity and a hint of knowing in his gaze. He had no doubt picked up on Virginia's interest in the young man's story, even if he did not know why.

"I am coming with you," Virginia blurted.

All went quiet as the two men stared, stunned by Virginia's outburst. She was shocked herself. The words sprang from her heart and out of her mouth without permission, but now that they were out, she had no intention of calling them back.

"I beg your pardon?" Charles questioned.

"I will accompany you and Richard on your journey."

"I know you have never adhered to social decorum, but you cannot be serious in your request," Robert fumed. "My unwed daughter, traveling the country with two unwed gentlemen, is not something I will allow to happen as long as there is still breath in my body!"

Virginia's mind raced, trying to find the right words to string together that would convince her father to allow her to go on the journey. Charles sat silently in his chair, amusement dancing in his eyes as he observed her. He would be of no assistance, but at least he was not shooting down her request as well. "Anna will accompany us!" Virginia asserted, proud of her solution.

"I will?" Anna chirped, her eyes wide with shock.

Virginia looked at the woman who'd sat silently in the corner until now, pleading with her to agree.

"I mean, I would be delighted to go," Anna stuttered.

"See, Father? All will be well. With a chaperone, my reputation will be safe."

"Your reputation would still be demolished. No."

Virginia refused to give up. Somehow, she would be on this trip. She had to be. Thinking, Virginia rose to her feet and paced the room.

Robert turned to Charles with an apologetic gaze. "Please, forgive my daughter. Her tongue has a tendency to get away from her at times."

"Do not apologize. I admit this entire exchange has been quiet amusing."

"I'm glad you think so," Robert said with an exasperated sigh and shake of his head. Turning to Virginia, he asked, "And what about your teaching?"

Darn the man for bringing that up. Her father would use the one thing he knew she loved to make her pause and think. To go on this trip would mean giving Mrs. Ruth her resignation. No longer being able to see Pearl and the other students.

But only temporarily. Virginia smiled when the thought popped into her mind. The trip would not last forever. It would probably only take a few weeks. "I will inform Mrs. Ruth of my short-term absence. She will understand once I tell her the reason. My position will be waiting for me once I return."

"The answer is still no!" her father barked, his peachy complexion beginning to resume the cherry coloring of earlier.

Virginia stewed, thinking of a solution. She had to go on this trip. "I will marry him," Virginia declared, cutting back into the conversation.

Again, the room went silent. Virginia walked back to her chair and sat. Three pairs of eyes were fixed on her, each with varying degrees of shock and concern.

This time there was no amusement in Charles's eyes when she met his gaze. He sat at attention in his chair, tea cup discarded and forgotten. "Surely, you jest."

"I do not. I will marry you if I am able to accompany you on this journey."

"It means that much to you to accompany us? Why?"

"It does. I..."

"Wait!" Robert cut in. "Virginia, do you truly mean it? You will be married?"

"Yes, Father. I will."

A wide, almost crazed smile spread across Robert's face. He had longed to hear such words from his daughter for so long. The fact that Charles was a lawyer and would be able to secure a comfortable life for Virginia added to his joy. "I will call for a priest."

"I beg your pardon, sir, but it is customary in nuptial arrangements for the groom to be in agreement with the wedding," Charles said, a hint of his previous amusement back in his tone.

"Why wouldn't you be? My daughter is beautiful, and you went through the trouble of finding our home and calling upon her without a proper invitation. It is obvious you fancy her. She will make a fine wife for you."

"Yes, but love—or at least a strong sense of liking—is usually required in these circumstances."

"Now you sound like her," Robert scoffed with a dismissive flick of his hand. "Love can be learned."

This situation was quickly passing down an avenue Virginia did not wish it to follow. "May I have a word with Charles in private, please?"

Charles arched a brow at her request. Virginia could only imagine what he was thinking. If she were in his position, she would probably deny the request and label the person mad.

"If your father will allow it, I will indulge you in a private conversation if for no other reason than to see what you can possibly come up with that you think will be sufficient to make me agree to marry you after one evening of dancing a year ago and a brief conversation over tea."

A flush of embarrassment crept over Virginia's cheeks. If she survived this day with a shred of dignity intact, she would praise the heavens.

"I will allow it. Come, Anna. We will give them a moment alone."

Eyes still wide, mouth agape, Anna rose from her chair and quietly followed Robert from the room.

Virginia waited until the door was closed before beginning her pleas to Charles. She smoothed her skirts to allow herself a moment to gather her courage. "I can only imagine how this request must sound to you. Quite possibly the strangest thing you have heard in a very long time."

"Possibly my entire life," Charles interjected, laughter in his voice.

"Yes, well." Virginia cleared her throat, eyes roaming the room before coming back to Charles. "Upon my marriage, my father will grant me a kind of inheritance of several thousand dollars. If you marry me and allow me to accompany you on this journey, I will give you five hundred dollars. You can keep it for yourself or use the funds to help with Mr. Taylor's abolitionist efforts."

Charles leaned back in his seat, quietly contemplating her words. He held his chin between his index finger and thumb, rubbing it as he stared off into space, lost in his thoughts.

Virginia was offering him a large sum of money, and she was glad he did not turn her offer down immediately. "And," she continued, unable to stand his silence, "after we have helped Richard, you may file for an annulment. You are a lawyer, so I assume you know how."

"That would ruin your reputation. You'd never be able to find a suitable husband after that," Charles replied, his head tilted as he studied Virginia. No doubt trying to see if she had fully thought this through or not.

"Doesn't matter." Virginia dismissed his statement with a flick of her hand. "I had no intention of acquiring one husband, let alone two. I have no qualms with spinsterhood, and upon my father's death, I will be an heiress."

Charles didn't immediately reply. He stared at Virginia, a smoldering heat burning in his gaze. "What if I don't wish for an annulment?"

Virginia swallowed hard. For the first time, doubt in the soundness of her plan crept in at the edge of her mind. She let out a laugh she hoped sounded more aloof than nervous. "You are a very humorous man. Now, do you accept my offer?"

"Why do you wish to come on this journey so badly?" Charles's intense gaze bore into hers, searching for answers.

The truth was, Virginia knew, but didn't know why, she wanted—no, needed—to come on this particular trip. She only knew that she did. Yes, she'd heard of other such stories of people in need of Conductors to lead their escape on the Underground Railroad. But something deep within her soul would not be at peace if she didn't participate in this trip. "Because my heart tells me it is something that I need to do."

"And you often listen to your heart?"

"I try to."

Charles tilted his head to the side again, searching Virginia's gaze. He must have found what he was looking for, because he gave one curt nod. "All right, then. We shall be married tomorrow before we leave. Tell your father to have the priest here at first light. I will come to collect you then."

"She will be ready," Robert announced as he marched back into the room. No doubt he had been listening at the door the entire time.

Charles let out a deep laugh as he rose to his feet. Robert came to a stop in front of him, offering his hand. Charles shook it, sealing their unwritten agreement.

Although it still hurt that her father was so willing to allow her to be married to a complete stranger, the pain was overshadowed by relief that, for once, her father's marriage schemes had worked in her favor.

"Sleep well, my lady," Charles said. "We have a long journey ahead of us. I bid you *adieu.*"

Virginia watched as Charles strolled out of the room, a slight skip in his step. Tomorrow, she would be Mrs. Charles Willcox, even if temporarily. A swarm of fluttering erupted in her stomach as the realization sank in.

This was an important moment. Her life would never be the same after tomorrow; she could feel it in her bones.

Chapter Eleven

HERE WERE NO BEAUTIFUL flowers, no special dress picked out specifically for the occasion, not even a crowd of well-wishers and friends.

This was not how Virginia had expected her wedding to go. Granted, in recent years, she hadn't expected to get married at all. But, back when she had allowed herself such girlish fantasies, this was not how she had imagined the day would unfold.

She did not expect to be standing in the parlor of her home, about to marry a virtual stranger, with only three guests: her father, a forced companion, and a man on a mission to save his woman. Nor a lawyer and half-asleep priest who had been reluctantly pulled from his bed before the sun rose, yawning his way through the marriage vows.

Virginia stared at the plain gold band on her left finger. This is what women coveted. To be eternally tied to a man. In fact, it was considered unnatural by some if a woman didn't desire marriage and children. So much so, if her father wasn't the man he was, Virginia might well have found herself in a mental institution by now for not wanting such things.

"Please sign here, madam," the priest said, interrupting her thoughts.

Virginia signed her name on the marriage certificate where the priest indicated. She was officially a married woman. Holding the quill suspended in the air above her signature, she stared at her name. She was officially someone else. Virginia Hatcher was no more; she was Virginia Willcox now.

The thought unnerved and excited her at the same time. This Virginia could be anyone she wanted. This Virginia could be brave, a fighter for those who could not fight for themselves. This Virginia *would* be those things.

"My condolences. I mean, my congratulations," the priest scrambled to say, fighting off another yawn. "I will take my leave now." He turned to leave without waiting for a reply.

"I believe it is my turn to collect signatures," the lawyer said as he laid a few papers in the same spot the marriage certificate had just been.

As her father had promised, he spoke with Charles before the wedding asking him to agree to an antenuptial contract. Charles had happily agreed to release his common law marital rights to her property, especially due to the temporary nature the marriage is based on.

Charles quickly signed where the lawyer indicated, but not before reading every word, of course. Once done, he placed his arm around Virginia's shoulders pulling her to his side. "Hello, Wife," he said with a cheeky grin.

Virginia laughed, shaking her head. She shrugged out of his embrace but didn't move away.

Excitement flowed through the room like a physical presence, each person with their own reasons for feeling it.

"Now that the formalities have been taken care of," Robert said, coming up to Virginia and Charles, "I have something for the both of you." He held two letters in his hands, extending one to Virginia and the other to Charles. "Wait until you have begun your travels before opening them."

They took the offered letters, each with their own sense of gratitude and curiosity about what they contained.

Robert wrapped his arms around Virginia, pulling her into a tight hug. When he released her, he kept her hands enclosed in his. "This may be an unorthodox arrangement, but something deep in my soul tells me that this is the right thing. You will find the love that you seek. I know you will."

Tears welled in Virginia's eyes. Something about the way her father had said those words sounded so final. She knew it was just her imagination, but she couldn't help the need to cherish this moment with her father, to engrave this rare show of affection onto her heart as if it was the last time she would have such a moment. "Thank you. I love you, Father."

"I love you, too, my darling."

Charles, Richard, and Anna waited patiently for Virginia and her father to finish their goodbyes. They had already lost precious travel time to hold the ceremony, and they needed to start their journey soon.

Releasing her father, Virginia turned to her now husband and their travel companions. "Shall we begin our adventure?"

"Yes, let the adventure begin," Charles replied with an excited smile.

"I've never been to the South before," Anna chimed in. "I admit I am a bit nervous, but thrilled to take part in this foray."

"And I thank you all for joining me. It truly means the world to me," Richard humbly said, a warm look of gratitude shining in his eyes. "Come now, the carriage awaits."

With their final goodbyes to Robert, the men collected their frock coats and the women their shawls, then headed out the door.

Charles strolled through the train car toward Virginia and Anna, who sat in their chairs chatting away. He had overseen the luggage to make sure the baggage smashers didn't live up to their names too much as they transported the small group's belongings. There wasn't much as they'd all packed a limited amount of clothing and toiletries to make for quicker travel. His luggage had gone in the sleeping car with Richard's.

Despite being a married couple by law, Virginia had made it very clear that they would not be engaging in the physical joys of their union. Thus, he found himself sharing a cramped sleeping car with a burly British man instead of his petite and delicate wife.

Virginia wore a jaded exterior, but Charles was eager to take on the challenge of stripping back her shields to explore the vibrant, passionate woman he saw lurking beneath the surface. And if he were wrong, and such a woman did not exist, he would file for annulment as she suggested.

"Ladies," he said in a smooth voice. He sat in the seat across from Virginia, since Anna occupied the one beside her.

Both ladies looked at him, one with a platonic softness in her gaze, the other with a more visceral appreciation. Charles smiled to himself, pleased with his effect on Virginia. "I hope I did not interrupt your conversation."

"Not at all," Anna chirped. "We were only discussing our excitement over this entire situation. We're helping a man rescue his love. How romantic and wonderful is it to be a part of such an experience?" She released a contended sigh, her eyes melting with soft contentment.

"I agree, it is a wonderful thing to be a part of. Although we met only days ago, I genuinely like Richard. I think he is an exceptional man to do what he is doing."

"I wouldn't call myself exceptional," Richard cut in as he walked up the aisle to the small group. He took the seat next to Charles. "Selfish, really. I can't live without Rose, and thus, I've dragged the lot of you into my dangerous mission to get her back. Hopefully, it shall not take much longer than a fortnight. I do not wish to take up too much of your time. And thank you all again for helping me achieve my heart's desire."

"Think nothing of it," Virginia replied. "It is truly our pleasure."

"Yes, well. It's you especially I'm grateful to, if not also a little confused by. Why would you marry a stranger to come on this journey?"

A slight blushed tinted Virginia's cheeks. The fact that her behavior was highly unusual wasn't lost on her. Despite the strangeness of it all, she did not shrink from Richard's question. "I've asked myself that very question many times over the past day. The only solution I've been able to come up with is that my motives are selfish, as well. I lost a very dear friend less than a year ago. She was a mulatress, the daughter of a Frenchman and an African woman. I wasn't able to save her, but this gives me the chance to help someone else. My heart yearns to do whatever I can, no matter how small."

Charles nodded his head in understanding, his respect for his wife growing. He understood her reasoning, even if it was a bit naïve and foolish.

"I can empathize with your pain," Richard said. "Thank you."

"Since we're all here, how about we discuss our plan?" Charles said. He sat up, craning his neck to glance around the train car. It was empty except for an older gentleman who sat engrossed in a newspaper at the other end. Charles leaned in, and everyone else followed suit.

It had taken him, Mr. Taylor, and Mr. Collins several hours to formulate their plan of action. With a bit of luck, Rose would have her freedom with little to no difficulty.

In a low whisper, he said, "As you all know, we are headed to Memphis, Tennessee. Once there, we will move quickly and stay less than a few hours. The day we arrive, we will check into a hotel, and you ladies will remain there until it's time to leave. That evening, Richard and I will sneak onto the farm to retrieve Rose.

"We will need you ladies to gather our belongings, then contact the conductor, Mr. Boyd. He will know where to meet us. All correspondences have been sent and arrangements made for our travels along the railroad. Mr. Boyd will transport us to our first station.

"After a day or so of hiding, we will continue onward, hopefully, with Rose's owner having given up the chase. She will be presented as Virginia's maid. I have also drawn up a set of papers stating that you are her owner in case they are needed."

Anna had leaned forward fractional degrees throughout his dialogue until she was practically falling out of her chair. Excitement and a touch of fear shone bright in her eyes. "My goodness, this is all so daring. I've never taken part in such an adventure. What is the possibility that we will be caught? What would be the consequences?"

"Now is probably not the best time to think of the consequences of being caught smuggling a slave to freedom," Charles stated with a soft chuckle. "Prior to agreeing to come along would have been better. All it will do now is serve to give the fears in our mind fuel to feast upon." Charles had never taken part in an operation of this capacity before. Normally, he was an agent, helping with planning and coordinating.

"Well, I, for one, do not fear what is to come. I am eager to face it," Virginia chimed in.

Despite her steely gaze, Charles could hear the slight quaver in her voice. "Fear is not entirely a horrible thing. It can be what keeps you aware, thus, keeping you alive. Make no mistake: our plan is solid, but our country is at war. This is a dangerous mission. It is wise to have some fear."

Richard shifted in his seat, his back rigid, eyes troubled. "I must confess something to you all."

All eyes turn to Richard. His gaze became jumpy, unable to face the scrutiny of the members of their small travel party.

A cold block of dread settled in Charles's stomach. This mission was dangerous enough; lies and surprises weren't something they could afford. "What is it?" he asked with caution.

"Rose is with child, nearing the end of her term."

An audible gasp sounded from the ladies, while Charles growled low in his throat. His mind immediately began assessing the complications and threats to their safety this would cause.

"Why didn't you tell us this before? This changes everything." Charles couldn't keep the accusation from his voice. If it were only he and Richard taking part in this journey, he wouldn't have been so concerned. But with Virginia and Anna in tow, they needed to remain cautious.

"I'm sorry. As I said, I am a selfish man. I needed the help to secure Rose's freedom before the child is born, and I couldn't jeopardize that."

Charles noticed Anna's eyebrows furrowing as she looked between the others. She didn't seem to understand the thick blanket of tension shrouding their group. "Pardon, but why is that a problem?"

"Because," Charles replied through clenched teeth, "she will not be able to travel for the length of time we intended. We will be much slower, and have to stop more frequently than planned. Not to mention the fact that she could give birth at any point. We have no plan in place should that occur."

Anna nodded her understanding. "That does present a rather cumbersome predicament."

"It does, but it isn't something we can't overcome," Virginia chimed in, her chastising gaze trained on Charles. "I, for one, feel compelled all the more to help Rose find her freedom. We now have the pleasure of helping two beautiful souls find their freedom. I am thrilled by the opportunity to take on such a noble endeavor."

It was clear that Charles wasn't going to win favor with anyone here by continuing to point out the obstacles they now faced. Virginia had thrown her lot in with Richard, no matter the cost, and she appeared determined to help free Rose. Again, Charles's respect for his wife grew. His naïve, tender-hearted wife.

"I'll think of a new plan. When we make it to the next railway station, I'll send a telegraph to Mr. Taylor with our change of circumstances. Now if you all will excuse me, I'll retire to my sleeping car for a mid-morning nap. Care to join me, Wife?"

Virginia's face went up in flames, causing it to match the bright red of her hair. She shot Charles a murderous glare for saying such a thing in front of the others. "No, thank you, Husband," she replied, derision dripping from every syllable of *husband*. "It's best you get used to an empty bed from the start, so that there's no mistake about what our marriage is, and what it is not."

Her words were meant to wound Charles, but all they did was amuse him further. He got under her skin. Good. "Very well then, Wife. I leave you in good company, and I bid you all *adieu*." Charles rose and squeezed past the others. This new development wasn't the best, but he would figure out a way around it. After all, he didn't think his wife would accept anything less from him.

Chapter Twelve

*T*HAT'S IT! Virginia sat up in her bed, unable to lay there for another minute. The need to move and be active clawed at her body until she could either obey and rise or go stark raving mad.

The bright, early morning sun shone through the window of the car, making it impossible to rest despite how desperately she wanted to cling to the land of sleep. She had finally found her way there a short while ago, and she'd tried to will herself to lay still and sleep, but her restless body would not cooperate.

Virginia and Anna had retired to their sleeping car rather early the night before. The early morning, rushed wedding and quick start to their travel had left her drained. A midday nap had sounded like a splendid idea when Charles mentioned it, but after his comment about joining him in his car, she wanted to stay awake the rest of the day to spite him.

Unfortunately for her, when Virginia was finally ready to retire, restful sleep would not come. Instead of the nothingness she desired, her mind was filled with visions of Charles, the devil of a man. Well, visions of *them* indulging in all the wicked things his eyes promised when he asked her to accompany him for a "nap."

Virginia looked over at Anna, who lay sound asleep in her bed. She had snuggled close to the wall, holding her pillow tightly against her chest. Small snores that sounded like oinks escaped her lips. Virginia smiled at her sleeping companion; even the woman's snores were cute.

Swinging her legs over the side of her bed, Virginia stretched to loosen the knots in her muscles. The soft bed was very comfortable, but foreign beds never provided the same restful sleep as your own.

As she stretched, her hand brushed against a piece of paper, sending it fluttering from the bed to the floor. It was the letter her father had given her. She'd placed it on the edge of her bed before her attempt to nap, in order to remind herself to read it. Good thing she knew herself so well, because she had already forgotten and its placement was perfect for her to bump into.

Virginia bent over and picked up the letter from the ground. She broke the seal and began to read.

My dearest daughter, I will keep this one short and say you have the tendency to be as stubborn as a mule. Alas, I must take responsibility for that flaw, because your mother was a saint. You have been presented with an opportunity to not only travel around the country, but to do it with your husband. Do not squander this opportunity. Talk with him and get to know him. Do not be bullheaded and hold onto this silly notion of spinsterhood you've adopted as of late. Who knows, you may find you enjoy the fellow. All my love. Your father.

Virginia gave a dismissive snort after reading the letter. She was not bullheaded. Well, maybe a little, but for good reason. She did not need or want a husband. She was perfectly happy with her own company. Folding the letter, Virginia shoved it under her pillow to attend to later. For now, she was in desperate need to walk. She opened the car door as quietly as possible so as not to disturb Anna and slipped out of the car.

Virginia stood in the doorway of the last car on the train, confused. Other travelers sat in their velvet-cushioned seats, chatting or reading various books and newspapers. Some had the curtains on their windows drawn to block out the sun, while others stared out at the endless expanse of land rushing by.

The car was nearly at capacity, but there was no Richard and no Charles. Virginia had started her search in first class, where they had been before, then made her way through the entire train. This was the last car, and still she'd seen no sign of them. Not that she was searching for them specifically to see Charles or because of her father's letter. She was simply bored, and they were her travel companions.

Where could they be? Apart from an act of the miraculous, Virginia couldn't imagine how two large men could vanish on a train speeding along the tracks.

As Virginia was about to give up her search and settle on reading a book from the train's small library, the door at the other end of the car opened, admitting a train attendant.

"Pardon me," Virginia said, walking up to the attendant. "I am in search of my travel companions. A tall, handsome man with blond hair and blue eyes, and a large man with reddish-brown hair and an English accent."

The attendant's face crumpled into a disgusted scowl before Virginia could finish her description of Charles and Richard. Had the gentlemen gotten into some sort of trouble while she and Anna were resting?

"Yes, I have seen those two," the attendant said in a disapproving tone. "They are in the Negro car. If those are your companions, I would encourage you to make wiser decisions about the company you keep." Nose in the air, the attendant turned on his heels, dismissing Virginia before she could make further inquiries.

Virginia felt no shame in knowing the men were in the colored car. In fact, she was proud of them and ashamed of herself for not thinking to look there when she couldn't find them anywhere else.

She wanted to follow after the attendant and tell him exactly that, but thought better of it. Apart from putting the haughty man in his place and receiving a modicum of satisfaction from that small act of vengeance, there was no real point. The attendant would still think them disturbed for wanting to associate with Negro people.

If only he knew the real reason behind their trip, he would probably drop dead from the scandal of it all. Either that, or attempt to turn them in to the authorities. Smiling to herself, Virginia went in search of the colored car.

"A stodgy old vulture told me I would find you here," Virginia said with a smile as she came up behind Charles and Richard. They sat at a small, rectangular table across from two smiling black men. Each had a set of cards in their hands, while a small pile of coins sat between them in the middle of the table.

"Hello there, Wife. I assume, from your description of the person, said vulture wasn't pleased with the place where they said you'd find us."

Virginia rested her hands on Charles's shoulders. She looked at the cards in his hands, then at his smiling face. The usual fluttering kicked up in her stomach. The man was handsome under the most ordinary circumstances, but when he was at ease and smiling, the man was downright gorgeous. "You would be correct in your assumption."

"Well, no matter. You have found us, and we are having a marvelous time. May I introduce you to Tom and Nathan? Gentlemen, this is my wife, Virginia."

"Pleasure, ma'am," the two men said in unison.

"The pleasure is mine," Virginia replied.

"All right, gentlemen, I see your nickels, and thus I fold. If you all will excuse me, I would like to chat with my wife before I lose any more money. We are newlyweds, and she doesn't know about my gambling addiction yet. I would like to keep it as such."

"Good idea," Tom replied with a chuckle. "Keep the vices hidden until after the first year. By then, you'll have put a baby in her an' she won't be goin' nowhere."

The men erupted into laughter, and Virginia couldn't help joining in. There would be no babies for them, but it was a funny sentiment nonetheless.

Charles placed his cards facedown on the table, pushing back to stand. "Come, let us find a seat where we can talk," he said to Virginia, motioning for her to follow.

They found two empty chairs in the middle of the car. These were not the soft, velvety cushioned chairs of first class; they were hard, wooden benches that required travelers to rise and walk about frequently or else face possible damage to their posterior and back.

Virginia and Charles settled onto the hard chairs, facing each other. They both proceeded to speak at the same time.

"Why did you—"

"Tell me about—"

They laughed at the blunder, both clamping their mouths shut.

"You first," Charles said.

"I saw your hand—you could have beat everyone and won. Why did you fold?"

"Sometimes life isn't about winning. It's about being humble and kind enough to allow others to have a much-needed victory. Yes, I could have beaten them, but they could use those coins more than I."

"Very true. But, in that case, they shouldn't have been gambling away the coins they did have," Virginia said with a raised eyebrow and a chiding smirk.

"Also true. But we are all human and subject to our vices. Sometimes, life has a way of treating us so poorly, we have to laugh to keep from crying and behave a little badly."

"Point well taken," Virginia replied. "Seeing as how we are now man and wife—no matter how short a time that may be—and since we are traveling across the country together, I thought it would be a good idea to learn more about each other."

"That sounds like a wonderful idea. I couldn't agree more."

"I suppose we can start with questions that are light in nature. Do you have a penchant for sweets?"

"I do not, actually. My mother never allowed me to have them as a lad, and now the taste doesn't sit well with me. Even a rich cake can be a bit much for my taste buds. What about yourself?"

"I love sugar in any form. Soleil would ridicule me endlessly about it. She was more like you when it came to sweets. She told me one day I would have no more teeth if I continued to eat such large quantities of the little butterscotch candies. But I would always smile in her face, butterscotch between my teeth, to taunt her with the fact that not a single tooth was missing." Virginia smiled at the memory of Soleil and her constant lectures. The smile quickly withered, as it always did when the joyful memories of her friends were overpowered by the sadness of loss.

"Tell me about Soleil," Charles said in a soft, soothing tone.

"She was the sister I never had and always wanted. Her father moved their family to America so he could pursue business opportunities for his shipping company. I met her when we were both shopping for dresses in the same boutique.

"The seamstress was rude to Soleil and her mother, ignoring them so she could serve me first, even though I came into the shop second. I gave her a good tongue-lashing and told her the color of my money was the same as theirs.

"Afterward, with a wide smile on her face, Soleil told me that we would be friends. Of course, I didn't mind being her friend, though, I have to admit that the matter-of-fact way she said it, coupled with the certainty in her eyes, made me wonder about the state of her mental faculties." Virginia released a small chuckle. "But that was Soleil. She had an open and caring heart that could make the grumpiest old man like her."

"She sounds like a phenomenal young woman."

"She was." Virginia placed her fingers to her cheek, where tears had slipped down her face without her realizing. She wiped them away and cleared her throat. "Yes, well. Tell me about yourself. Why did you decide to practice law in service of people of color?"

Charles pulled out the locket he always carried with him. "I guess you could say I do it for similar reasons—for someone I loved." He opened the locket and handed it to Virginia. Inside were two pictures: one of a mulatto woman with beautiful bronze skin, and the other of a much fairer woman who could pass for white. Both were stunning beauties with the dignified carriage of royalty.

"That is my grandmother, and that is my mother," Charles said, pointing to each woman. "My grandmother was born a slave, and she gave birth to my mother when she was sixteen. My mother's father was one of the overseers. My grandmother lived a harsh life but never complained. The only thing she ever asked for from life was that her daughter would be safe. Unfortunately, my mother was a stunning beauty and attracted the notice of several men.

"On my mother's fifteenth birthday, she was cornered by one of the farmhands. She fought with everything she had and got away. That night, my grandmother collected her distraught daughter, packed up the little she owned, and ran. Without the help of the brave men and women who risk their lives every day to ferry slaves to freedom, my grandmother and mother would not have made it north. My mother would not have met my father, and I would not be here."

Virginia listened, shocked and riveted by his story. She had so many questions for him. "Your father married your mother, knowing she was a Negro?"

"No, my father never knew. She told him that my grandmother was her maid. I wish I could say that my father would have been understanding had he known, but I'm not so sure. He did love her with all his being. My mother was an incredible woman. She died when I was thirteen but told me the truth about her and my grandmother and gave me this locket before she passed."

Virginia threw her arms around Charles and pulled him into a tight hug. Stunned, he hesitated for a moment before wrapping his arms around her and pulling her into his lap.

"I'm sorry."

"Thank you," Charles whispered into the crook of her neck.

They sat wrapped in each other's arms, neither saying a word. Tears flowed over Virginia's cheeks, but she didn't try to wipe them away. She didn't know who the tears were for...Soleil. Charles. His family. Herself.

One day, the pain of division would be gone from the

world. Love would prevail, and all people would be unified. She believed it with all her heart. She needed to believe it.

Chapter Thirteen

THERE WAS NOTHING MORE mesmerizing than the beauty of nature untouched by man. Miles of vegetation flew past the train as Charles stared out the window.

After his conversation with Virginia, he had gone back to the sitting car to be alone and think. He had never shared his heritage with anyone else, not even Mr. Taylor. By no means was he ashamed of his mother and grandmother. In fact, he celebrated their beauty. But the paleness of his skin was a blessing and a gift he wanted to use to help others.

He had to protect his secret and be careful with whom he shared it. Any person with even one ancestor of African heritage was classified as Negro. Being found out would demolish his chances of practicing law for the betterment of all people. And, right now, the world needed more men willing to do just that.

With the information he had shared, Virginia could tear down his entire world. But he knew she wouldn't; the way she'd held him and cried in his arms reassured him of that.

"Excuse me, sir. Is there anything I can get for you?"

Charles looked up at the attendant smiling down at him. The young man had a genuinely pleasant disposition. "Yes. A Scotch, please."

"Make that two," Richard said, coming up the aisle.

"Right away, gentlemen," the attendant replied with a small nod of his head.

Richard took the seat across from Charles.

"We arrive in Chattanooga tomorrow," Charles said. "I'm not sure if there will be a reply to my telegraph waiting for us, but I gave Mr. Taylor all our stops along the way, so we should hear something back from him soon."

"Excellent. Thank you. And, again, I apologize for not telling you about Rose's condition." Richard cast a remorseful gaze at Charles, who stared back unmoved.

Charles cocked his head to the side, studying the man before him, debating how he should deliver his next words. "I want you to understand something," Charles said in a firm, level tone. "When I initially agreed to assist you on this mission, my life was in a different place than it is now. Nothing that has happened since then has been planned, but I must admit I like this unforeseen turn of events. With that said, I need you to know that I won't tolerate any more lies or surprises from you. If you do anything to put Virginia's life in danger, I will have no choice but to break our arrangement and possibly your legs. Do we understand each other?"

"Yes," Richard confirmed with a nod. A wide smile spread across his lips. "If the roles were reversed, I would tell you the same thing. So, your wife is growing on you, I see."

"That she is, the little spitfire. One minute, she glares at me as if she wishes my death, and the next, she's wrapping me in a hug that could cure any ailment."

"I understand; Rose is the same way."

"How did the two of you meet?"

Richard's smile grew wider as he slipped into the memory of meeting the one and only Rose Fletcher. "I was in Memphis on holiday a few years back. The ale is cheap, and the women loose," he said with a wink. "I was completely sloshed and arguing with a bloke about something I can no longer recall as I stumbled out of a whorehouse. I found myself hungry and meandered into the market searching for food. I wasn't paying attention and ran right into her, knocking her over.

"She cursed me out good and proper, and I fell in love with her right then and there. Although, it was probably the alcohol talking, for the most part. When I sobered up, I asked around as discretely as possible and found out where she lived. It took me an entire month to get her to talk to me, but it was a month well spent."

"She sounds like just the woman you need."

"She is, in every way. When I found out she was expecting our child, I didn't think my heart would be able to contain all the joy. I've wanted to take her back to England since she first told me she loved me, but Rose is a stubborn one. She was afraid of getting caught, but our child has given her courage."

Richard smiled to himself, and Charles watched him closely. What would it be like to feel that? To know that the woman you loved would be bringing the child you created together into the world.

"Here you are, gentlemen," the attendant said as he came

back with a tray holding their drinks. He bent low so Richard and Charles could take their drinks.

"Thank you."

"Thanks."

The attendant gave a small bow and smile before turning to leave again. Charles took a sip of his Scotch, enjoying the smooth burn as it went down.

"So, what is your plan to win over your wife?" Richard asked with a knowing smile.

"I could pretend I don't understand the meaning of your question, but since we're both intelligent men, I will not insult us in such a way. My answer is, therefore, that I have no plan."

Richard chuckled into his Scotch. "Then today is your lucky day. As repayment for helping me free my wife, I will help you win the heart of yours."

"You think yourself an expert in such matters?"

"Winning over Rose was like trying to sell ice during an English winter. If I can get that girl to love me, I must know a little something. That is, if you want to win her over."

Charles mulled that question over. Did he want to win Virginia? The ever-present, logical portion of his brain presented the fact that he barely knew her. The other portion returned that that was part of the process of winning her over—learning more about her and what she was made of. "All right, then. Impart your wisdom upon me."

Richard leaned in as if the information he was about to share was more precious than the crown jewels and not to be missed. "Here is what you do," he whispered. "Tomorrow, on the steamboat..."

Chapter Fourteen

IRGINIA LEANED ON THE rail of the steamboat, looking out over the water. Waves swelled in the boat's
wake, starting rough and wild before they calmed
to soft ripples as they spread toward a distant shore Virginia
couldn't see through the darkness.

The reflection of stars glittered on the water, giving it an
ethereal glow. A warm southern breeze floated off the water
washing over her. This was the kind of evening poets wrote
about—one in which, if fairies truly existed, they would dance
upon the water, casting the shimmer of their magic over star-
crossed lovers.

The fresh, open air on the water was a welcomed relief
from the cramped confines of the train. Virginia wished they
could travel this way for longer than a few hours. But the
journey was almost over, which Virginia was grateful for.

"I was told to give these to you." Anna walked up to
Virginia, two beautiful red roses in her hands. She held them
out to Virginia, a wide, jubilant smile on her face.

"Where did these come from?" Virginia asked in confusion.

"Read the note!" Anna sang with excitement as she pointed to the item in question.

Virginia picked up the note tucked between the roses and lifted it out as slowly as she could. She erupted in laughter when Anna's smile fell, while she deliberately drew out opening the note.

"What are you doing? Hurry up—open it," Anna said, waving her arms to hurry Virginia along.

Virginia barked a peal of laughter at the other woman's antics. She smelled the roses, closing her eyes to bask in the scent. When the sound of Anna's tapping foot reached her ears, Virginia opened her eyes and gave her an innocent smile. "I thought this gift was for me. I can enjoy it at any pace I like."

"Read the note, or so help me, I will sit on you while you sleep."

Virginia laughed harder but quickly opened the note. She scanned the letter, reading the contents to herself.

"Out loud!" Anna shouted, throwing up her hands and rolling her eyes.

"It's a note from my husband." Virginia clutched the note close to her chest, away from Anna's prying eyes.

"Yes, I know that. He's the one who told me to give it you."

"Notes between husbands and wives are generally private."

"Sit. On. You."

Virginia laughed so hard her stomach began to hurt. Boundaries were something Anna clearly didn't understand, but that only served to inflame the mischievous side of Virginia that enjoyed keeping Anna in suspense.

"All right. It says, 'My dearest Virginia, a part of me would like to write you the sweetest sonnet or letter of love that has ever been written. I would like to fill it with loving words that would make the angels in heaven weep. But, alas, I was given you for a wife. As such, I know that you have already condemned me for calling you 'my dearest,' and frilly words would only serve to make you avoid me at all costs. So, my radiant wife, I will simply say nothing at all. But know that my thoughts of you are filled with words such as divine, stunning, brilliant, and kind. From my heart to yours. Your husband, Charles.'"

Virginia sighed as she finished reading the letter. Never before had she received such a letter that spoke to her soul and made her want to shout with joy. Her heart warmed, and she yearned to read the note again and again.

"Lovely," Anna said with a sniffle, wiping the tears from her cheeks. Blotchy red spots covered her round face and cheeks as she fanned herself to make the tears stop. "That was truly marvelous."

"Yes, it was." Virginia smiled to herself. *Drat and tarnation.* Charles was good. Very good. With one note, he made Virginia yearn for things she shouldn't want. He made her want him.

"Oh! Before I forget," Anna said, wiping the last tears from her face, "I was supposed to tell you to go to the boiler deck."

"What's on the boiler deck?" Virginia asked, crossing her arms. She tilted her head to the side, narrowing her eyes to give Anna the most intimidating stare she could muster.

Anna stared right back, hands on her hips. "I hope you don't expect me to answer that. Go and find out."

Left with little choice as Anna shooed her away, Virginia turned and did as instructed, making the short walk to the boiler deck.

Oil lamps placed around the deck greeted Virginia when she ascended the stairs. They cast off their soft light, wrapping the area in a warm, cozy glow. A man sat in a chair off to the side near the railing, a violin resting in his lap.

Charles stood in the middle of the floor, back rigid, hands clasped behind his back. His foot bounced, tapping the floor, seemingly unable to be still. If he were any other man, Virginia would say he looked nervous, but surely, Charles was not prone to falling victim to sentimental emotions.

"Hello, Wife."

"Hello, Charles. What is the meaning of all this?" Virginia gestured to the lanterns and violinist.

Charles stepped toward her, not stopping until they were inches apart. Virginia wanted to take a step back to restore the distance between them, but refused to give Charles the satisfaction of knowing how he affected her.

She couldn't think straight with Charles so close. Her mind filled with silly notions and questions, such as what would it feel like to be kissed by him? And the yearning to be held tightly in his arms again. Her fingers tingled with the desire to reach out and stroke his soft blond hair.

"This is my attempt to win over my wife."

Charles signaled the violinist, who began to play a slow waltz. Before Virginia could protest, he removed the roses from her hand placing them on the ground. Then he placed one of her hands on his shoulder, wrapped his hand around her waist, took her other hand in his, and began twirling her around the deck. "Do you remember the first time we danced?"

"I do." Virginia smiled, remembering the night she first laid eyes on Charles. As soon as she saw him, she made it her mission to introduce herself. Not only because he was the most handsome man at the party, but also because of his eyes. They were the eyes of a humble and kind man; a fact that Virginia could now confirm without a shadow of a doubt.

"You marched up to me and dragged me onto the dance floor," he said.

"I knew what I wanted, and that was to dance with you," Virginia quipped, giving Charles a saucy smile. It quickly faded as their current reality slammed back into her. "But that was a different girl. Charles, you can't win my heart. I won't let you."

"Why ever not?"

"Because...I just can't."

Charles pulled her in closer. He leaned in, capturing her gaze, and whispered, "I won't stop pursuing you. I saw even back then that you were special, but I foolishly let you slip away. I won't squander my second chance."

Virginia averted her gaze. She couldn't let him see what those words did to her, how much she cherished them. "You will be wasting your time."

"We shall see."

Charles spun her around faster, ending the conversation. They continued to dance in each other's arms, never taking their eyes off the other.

Virginia basked in the warmth of his embrace and the tender way he watched her. If she were ever to allow herself to fall in love, it would be with a man like Charles. If only.

Chapter Fifteen

Tennessee, April 1862

VIRGINIA STRETCHED IN THE tiny bed of the sleeping car. Rays of light from the early morning sun shone through the tiny gap in the curtains.

Giddy anticipation took over her mind as the last remnants of sleep wore off. Today was the day they would arrive in Memphis.

After nearly five days of traveling over fifteen hundred miles, Virginia was more than ready to plant her feet on solid ground that wasn't moving. They had traveled by railroad, steamboat, stagecoach, and now finally were on the last leg. In a few hours, the train ride would be over.

"Good morning," Anna beamed, sitting up in her bed. She placed the book she'd been reading in her lap and smiled at Virginia.

"Good morning," Virginia sleepily returned with a yawn. As she stretched one last time, Virginia's eyes landed on a tray of food on the small table between their beds. The smell of coffee tickled her nose, making her want to moan in apprecia-tion. Fresh fruits, cheese, and bread were neatly arranged on the tiny plate. "Did you get this for me?"

"No, Charles brought it by not too long ago. I wanted to wake you so that you could give your thanks, but he told me to allow you to sleep. Such long journeys can be exhausting."

Virginia's heart swelled, as it had many times over the past few days. Ever since their night on the steamboat, Charles had made it his mission to do little things to break through the armor Virginia had placed around her heart. Unfortunately, it was working.

Virginia popped a piece of cheese into her mouth, chewing around her smile. "I will thank him when I see him."

"Speaking of which, we should hurry and get dressed. We have to meet the gentlemen to discuss the amendments to our plan."

Ah, yes. Charles had received a telegraph from Mr. Taylor in LaGrange before they boarded this train.

Virginia threw back the covers and stood. "Well, no time for dallying. Out of bed with you," she playfully chided. "Re-ally, Anna, you can't lay about all day." Virginia stood over Anna's bed, a mock glare on her face, as if she were not the one who had been asleep until moments ago.

"How thoughtless of me," Anna replied in a sarcastic tone. Rising from the bed, she stuck out her tongue and tossed a pillow at Virginia. Both women giggled as it hit her shoulder and bounced off, landing on the floor.

Virginia moved about the tiny room, unable to keep still. She pulled out her dress, packed up her belongings, checked and re-checked to make sure she hadn't missed anything, all while laughing and occasionally pulling Anna into an unexpected hug.

Anna laughed along, feeding off her excitement. The anticipation was almost too much. Today, they would defy an entire segment of their nation. Today, they would play their small part in changing someone's life. Today, they would take part in reshaping history.

"Good morning, ladies," Richard said. He and Charles rose to their feet when Virginia and Anna walked up to their seats.

"Good morning, gentlemen." Virginia and Anna returned the greetings before taking the available seats across from the men.

Once they were seated, Charles pulled a folded piece of paper out of the breast pocket of his vest and held it up before them. "I received word from Mr. Taylor that new stations have been arranged for us. We will still rendezvous with Mr. Boyd when we arrive in Memphis, and he will escort us to the first station. I've been informed that the station master's wife has helped deliver babies of other families in their town. Should the need arise, she will be more than happy to assist Rose."

Charles directed his last statement at Richard, who nodded his head in understanding. "Due to Rose's delicate condition, we will stay at our first station for three days. Hopefully, her owner will give up the chase sooner rather than later, but it gives us a longer window for him to do so. That will afford us the ability to travel to the second station with more peace of mind that we will not need to add the strain of long periods of travel for Rose."

"Excellent!" Richard slapped his pant leg, a wide grin on his face.

"Most of our travel until North Carolina will be by wagon. Once we make it to North Carolina, we will purchase train tickets to travel back to New York."

"And once we reach New York, I will bid you all *adieu.* Rose and I shall sail to England." Richard's joyful smile softened. He leaned forward, taking one of Virginia's and one of Anna's hands in his to give them a light squeeze. "Again, thank you all for your assistance on this journey. To be able to hold Rose in my arms and wake up to her smiling face every morning is a blessing for which I cannot properly express my gratitude."

Virginia gave his hand a gentle squeeze in return, patting it with her free hand. "You truly have nothing to thank us for," she replied with a soft smile. "I invited myself along and will not play a major role in the actual rescue. I thank you for allowing us to come along."

Charles's heart filled with joy and gratitude as he watched the exchange. These were his friends. This was his wife. Together, they were about to accomplish something amazing. "All right, everyone. We should be pulling into Memphis shortly. When we do, I will send word to Mr. Boyd of our arrival. Be very careful and speak to as few people as possible. Understood?"

Everyone nodded their heads in understanding. Each wore varying expressions of excitement, nervousness, and anticipation. The time was now upon them to risk their lives to save someone else's.

Virginia sat on the bench of the carriage Charles had secured for them wringing her hands, unable to keep them still. They were finally here. No one spoke as the carriage jostled along its bumpy path.

She pulled back the curtain to look out at the expanse of lush green land as they passed. This was Memphis, Tennessee. It was absolutely gorgeous. The closer they came to the heart of the city more and more buildings and business sprouted up.

Stories told about the war's effect on the South generally included women wearing faded dresses in desperate need of replacement. Men wearing pants with knees so threadbare, resulting holes had been patched multiple times.

Such was not the case here. This was a place that had been blessed by abundant cotton crops, a well-equipped system of railroads and steamboats to carry them to buyers, and the wealth that such conditions created.

The coach soon pulled onto Main Street. People milled about entering and exiting stores along the street. Children clung to their mothers' skirts as they laughed or chewed on sweet treats.

Virginia drew in a deep breath when the coach began to come to a stop in front of the hotel that would serve as their temporary quarters. Each second that passed, each event that happened this day brought them closer to the climax of their purpose here. Closer to the point where they would succeed or fail in saving someone's life. That was a heavy weight to bear.

When the wagon came to a complete stop, Virginia breathed a sigh of relief. The stress of their mission and being confined to moving metal boxes and tight rooms for days left her restless. She planned to go for a walk with Anna while they awaited the arrival of the evening.

"Wife, I would like to stretch my legs. Would you care to join me?" Charles must have read her mind.

"Yes, of course."

"Excellent. Richard would you mind seeing to our bags and making sure Anna is settled in her room?"

"I would be delighted to," Richard replied with a small smile. The abundance of merriment Virginia had seen from him until this point was now subdued.

"Thank you," Anna said to Richard in a tight voice.

Virginia was grateful when the coachman opened the door and extended his hand to help her and Anna down. The tension hanging over them all was like a suffocating dark cloud.

Charles and Richard hopped out after them. Anna walked into the hotel without her usual cheerful goodbye as Richard helped the driver with the bags.

Charles extended his arm to Virginia, which she took, allowing him to lead her down the street with no particular destination in mind.

"How are you feeling?" Charles asked.

"My honest answer is nervous and a little afraid."

"As you should be. This is a dangerous mission, but I have a good feeling about it."

Virginia tightened her grasp on Charles's arm and leaned her head against his shoulder. She cast her eyes to the ground, lost in thought. What words could she use to convey what she needed to say next?

"Charles, if anything happens tonight..."

"No!" Charles interrupted with a firm reprimand. "I will not allow you to speak such words. Tonight will be a success. Something we can tell our children about, and they, their children."

Charles flashed Virginia his sensual smile that always sent her heart fluttering. She couldn't help but return the smile. She also didn't miss his comment about the future children they would have together, but chose not to reply.

"Here," Charles said, reaching into his pocket and pulling out his locket. "Hold on to this for me. Return it after Richard and I return from retrieving Rose."

Charles placed the tiny locket in Virginia's open palm and closed her fingers over it. Virginia sucked in a quick breath as she stared at her closed fist. Charles was entrusting her with the one thing in the world that meant the most to him. Virginia was both honored and frightened by that.

"I will keep it safe," Virginia said in a voice soft with wonder.

"I know you will."

Charles leaned in and placed a quick kiss on Virginia's cheek. The urge to place her hand over the spot he kissed built inside Virginia, but she refrained from doing so in front of him.

"Yes, well, I guess you should go and contact Mr. Boyd. I can see myself back to the hotel. I'll be waiting on your return."

"As you wish, Wife. I shall return soon."

Charles released Virginia's hand and walked away to accomplish his task. She watched until he was out of sight. "Please, watch over him and watch over us all tonight," Virginia whispered into the air, hoping that her request was heard by someone.

Chapter Sixteen

ARKNESS SO THICK CHARLES could hardly see his hand in front of his face encased them. Crickets chirped their nighttime symphony in the distance, creating a serene melody in stark contrast to the rhythmic hammering of his heart.

Faint beams of moonlight penetrated the thick foliage of the trees, guiding them toward their destination. Charles and Richard had been picking their way through the forest for the past twenty minutes.

Per Richard's assurances, a large white house Charles assumed was the McPhearson Plantation soon came into view. No lights shone inside the house, and Charles detected no movement.

"She will be waiting by the back door in the kitchen," Richard whispered over his shoulder. Charles gave a slight nod in understanding.

They made their way out from the cover of the trees and onto the open lawn. Charles scanned the area, alert to the smallest possible movements. Nothing seemed out of the ordinary thus far, but, for some reason, that only served to put Charles on edge even more.

The night seemed to quiet down the closer they came to the house. Charles gave silent thanks when they reached the back door without incident. He continued to watch their surroundings as Richard lightly tapped on the door.

Instead of the feminine voice he'd expected, low growls answered the knocking. Richard and Charles froze, staring between each other. Where was Rose, and why had there been no mention of dogs?

Richard rose on his toes to peer through the glass pane at the top of the door. "I don't see Rose," he whispered to Charles as he moved his head side to side, scanning the inside of the kitchen. "Wait! There she is."

Charles came to stand by Richard at the door, looking through the window. A beautiful woman with russet brown skin and a large puff of curly black hair tied back in a dull gray headwrap stood just on the other side of the door clutching her rounded belly.

Two dogs barked and clawed at the door, blocking her escape. Fear and uncertainty shone through her round eyes as she tried to quiet the animals. Charles noted that, apart from making noise that would wake others in the house, the dogs were no threat to Rose's safety. They paid her no mind as they focused on the intruders on the opposite side of the door.

"Rose," Charles whisper-shouted through the window. "They know you. They will not harm you. Distract them. Give them something to eat, then open the door slowly to make your escape."

"Yes, sir," Rose replied. She waddled around the kitchen as fast as her protruding belly would allow, gathering slices of dried meat left over from the evening meal.

Charles and Richard both looked up as the soft glow of a candle came to life, shining through the window of a room on the upper flower. Richard cursed under his breath, body rigid, ready to leap into action. "Hurry, my love. Someone is coming," he called through the window.

Rose whistled low and dangled the dry meat out beside her to get the dogs' attention. Intruders forgotten, the dogs darted toward Rose then to the left where she tossed the meat. As they devoured the snack, Rose waddled toward the door a smile on her face. Richard smiled back through the window, no doubt ready for this to be behind them and to have Rose safely in his arms.

Charles moved to take a step back to allow Rose room to exit, but stopped when he noticed the smile slip from her face. She stood on the other side of the door but didn't open it. He and Richard looked through the window but couldn't see what was making Rose hesitate.

"He locked the door. He never locks the door. I don't have a key. I can't open it," Rose cried in a shrill voice.

"Don't panic, Rose. We will get you out of there," Richard replied in an even tone, trying not to scare her further.

"I hear someone coming," she cried. Tears streamed down her face as she began banging on the door.

"We need to get her out of there," Richard bellowed, his chest heaving up and down.

"I know, my friend. Calm down. Let's think." Everything

was happening so fast. Charles could barely pull his thoughts together into a cohesive string. Rose's soft cries and Richard's angry breathing tore at his heart.

Ignoring Charles, Richard punched the door causing a small crack to form in the wood.

That's it. "We have to break down the door. Together, we will ram into it," Charles said.

Richard immediately backed up, tilting his shoulder down, ready to slam into the door with all the force his body could muster.

"Rose. Back away from the door," Charles instructed.

When she did as he asked, Charles backed up next to Richard. He gave a slight nod, and they ran at the door full force. Their shoulders slammed into the door, but apart from causing the door to crack, their effort did nothing.

"What's going on down there," a voice called from deep within the house.

"Hurry," Rose pleaded. "He's coming."

"Again," Richard bellowed.

They backed up and slammed into the door a second time. Still, the door didn't open.

"Again," Richard ordered.

Charles hesitated. Perhaps they needed to come up with a new plan. He took a step back and took several deep breaths to calm his mind enough to think.

Richard, however, fueled by rage and adrenaline, backed up and slammed into the door again. Then, again. When it still did not budge, he let out a roar as he began kicking the door repeatedly.

"Here. Use this."

Charles whipped around the see Virginia running up behind them, an axe clutched in her hands. "What are you doing here?"

"No time," she replied, handing the axe to Richard.

He snatched it from her hands and began swinging it at the handle of the door. After three strikes, the handle splinted from the door and fell to the ground.

"Wait," Charles barked, grabbing Richard's arm before he could swing the door open wide. "The dogs. Rose, open the door just enough so you can squeeze through."

Even though the dogs were still occupied with the meat she had laid out for them, Charles wanted to take no chances. Obeying his command, Rose inched the door open just wide enough for her small rounded body to fit through.

"You, there. Stop!" shouted a portly older man as he ran from the front of the house toward the kitchen. The glow of his lamp grew brighter. "Bruce, Sadie," he shouted to the dogs, "get 'em."

The animals immediately obeyed their master's command, forgetting about the scraps of meat left for them to devour.

Throwing caution to the wind, Richard snatched open the door and yanked Rose through it. She teetered on her feet and would have fallen over if not for his strong arm banded around her waist keeping her upright. Richard quickly slammed the door shut and shoved the blade of the axe between the hinges and the door frame to jam it.

"Let's go," Charles shouted as he clasped Virginia's hand in his own.

They took off running into the night toward the rendezvous point where Mr. Boyd would be waiting. From behind them, loud barking and the angry shouts of Rose's owner echoed through the night. Not looking back, they ran full speed into the cover of the trees.

"No, not that way. This way," Virginia said as she dug her heels into the ground. Their still interlocked hands caused Charles to jerk to a stop beside her and Richard and Rose to stumble to a stop before crashing onto their backs.

"This is the way to..."

"No," Virginia cut him off. "Mr. Boyd and Anna are waiting with the wagon this way." Virginia pointed to the left and in the opposite direction than they were headed.

Charles's uncertain gaze followed her finger. Logic told him that Virginia would not jeopardize everyone's safety, including her own, by giving them bad information. Yet another, smaller, part of him wanted to hold on to the plan he knew to be true.

"We switched the meeting place to a closer location when I decided to help."

"Alright. Lead the way," Richard said, not wanting to waste more time. He turned and ran in the direction Virginia indicated. Rose waddled beside him struggling to keep up. Her feet continued to stumble along the dirt path, threatening to send her tumbling to the ground. Richard scooped her up in his arms and took off running at a faster pace.

Charles and Virginia followed closely on his heels. They ran blindly through the forest guided only by the light of the moon and stars that penetrated the leaves and branches above them. It didn't take long for the faint glow of a lantern to shine up ahead. Charles pumped his legs faster, eating away the distance. Safety was within reach.

"Oh, thank goodness!" Virginia breathed on a relieved sigh.

"Come, come. Hurry now," Mr. Boyd beckoned from the driver's seat of the wagon. Anna sat beside him eyes wide and mouth slightly ajar as she watched them sprint toward her. The small group didn't slow down until they reached the wagon.

"I've got you." Anna reached down, helping to pull the ladies into the cart. The men leaped in behind them. Mr. Boyd snapped the reigns, sending the horses into a gallop as soon as they were in.

Barking and the shouting of several voices carried on the wind a short distance behind them. They didn't have much time. Mr. Boyd needed to put more distance between them and the plantation quickly. He yanked on the reigns, forcing the horses to make a hard left. The wagon teetered on its wheels, threatening to tip over. With a hard crash, it again resumed moving on all four wheels.

They continued to gallop full speed through the dimly lit forest. The wagon jumped and shook, mercilessly tossing everyone about.

"Don't worry," Mr. Boyd shouted over his shoulder. "We will lose them soon."

Richard held on to Rose, and Charles held on to Virginia as tightly as they could to keep the women steady on the volatile ride.

The low gurgling of running water soon reached their ears. Mr. Boyd spurred the horses on, guiding them into the water. They sunk deeper into the river until the water crept into the wagon bed. Charles gave thanks for its calm flow.

The horses cut through the water with little struggle. It didn't take long for them to reach the other bank and return to dry land.

"We should be safe now," Mr. Boyd said, but he didn't slow the pace of the horses. "The water will throw the dogs off our scent. It's not a long journey to the first station, so y'all will be in hiding soon."

"Thank you," Richard and Charles respond at the same time.

Everyone relaxed, allowing the tension of all that had recently transpired to ease from their weary bones. No one would feel completely at ease, however, until they reached their destination.

"Thank you," Richard said as he extended his hand to Charles.

"You're very welcome," Charles replied, taking the offered hand in a firm handshake.

"Thank you all for rescuing me," Rose said with a warm smile. She snuggled closer to Richard's side, circling her arms around his waist.

With a contented sigh, Virginia rested her head against Charles's shoulder. He looked down at her, grateful for her safety and equally upset that she had disobeyed the plan and risked her life in such a reckless way. But he would discuss that with her later. For now, Charles only wanted to allow everyone to bask in the relief of accomplishing their mission. He closed his eyes and leaned his head back against the hard wooden wall of the wagon. Tonight was a success and that's all that mattered.

Chapter Seventeen

FOUR DAYS. FOUR LONG, stressful, tiresome days they've been hiding in the house of Mr. and Mrs. Jamison. The plan had been to stay at this first station at most three days, then move on to their next stop. But Mr. McPhearson had not let up the search as they'd hoped.

Their small party spent the most part of the first day huddled together in the cramped hidden cellar under the home when a man had come by asking about Rose. Mr. McPhearson had men with dogs on constant patrol. They worked in shifts, night and day, so that someone was always on the lookout. Traveling the long distance to the next destination with no protection would result in the capture of their small party in no time.

Charles, Virginia, Richard, and Rose were in the small home's sitting room waiting for another day to pass. The curtains were drawn shut, blocking out the sunlight Charles had begun to miss over the past few days.

Anna was out in the garden helping Mrs. Jamison with the crops. Of all of them, she had the most freedom, although, it was used to help around the house.

Virginia had wanted to help as well to show her appreciation for their hospitality, but it was decided that it would be too risky. One unannounced stranger the Jamisons could explain away if anyone asked. Two would be more difficult. It had been decided that if anyone asked they would say Anna was Mr. Jamison's niece.

Rose and Virginia sat on the sofa together keeping themselves busy with needlework. Richard sat in a chair he pulled next to the sofa reading a book. His hand rubbed up and down Rose's back. He hadn't let her out of his sight since the rescue, and his hands constantly touched her as if he needed reassurance she was real.

"Something is not right here," Charles stated as he paced back and forth across the small space of the room. His long-clipped steps took him back and forth across the room in a few strides.

Everyone stopped what they were doing and glanced at Charles. Richard lowered his book to his lap, guilt shining in his eyes as he looked at Charles.

"What aren't you telling us?" Charles growled low.

Rose looked at Charles then Richard, a silent plea in her gaze.

Charles's eyes narrowed on them, the muscles in his body coiling with tension. They were hiding something.

Virginia put down her needlework, silently watching the other couple; her brows furrowed in confusion.

Richard took Rose's hand in his, then released a heavy sigh. "Rose stole the accounting ledgers for McPhearson's plantation as a means of additional protection. His plantation has been suffering financially for the past several years. He owes the bank a large sum, and they will repossess his property if they find out the true state of his finances. That is why he has not given up looking for her," Richard confessed.

"What?!" Charles bellowed.

Before Richard could reply, the front door opened admitting a laughing Mrs. Jamison and Anna. They walked toward the sitting room chatting away. The smiles fell from their lips and their conversation came to an abrupt halt as soon as they entered the room.

Charles stood glaring down at Richard, his hands balled into fists at his side. The tension radiating through the room was so thick it became its own physical presence.

"What's going on?" Mrs. Jamison asked.

"Tell her," Charles barked.

Richard stood tall, accepting and owning his deception. "We have information that can be used to extort Mr. McPherson, which is why he hasn't given up his search for Rose. He wants the information back."

Anna and Mrs. Jamison gasped, eyes widening at his revelation.

"Oh dear!" Mrs. Jamison said, clutching her hand to her chest. "You will need to leave immediately. I'm so sorry, but this brings in a new level of danger to our home that I cannot allow. We will help you make arrangements, but you will need to leave soon."

"Please, Mrs. Jamison," Virginia begged. "Give us time to make a proper plan."

"I'm sorry, dear, but your stay is now over. I heard there is a Union encampment in Shiloh. It's not too far, and they will be able to provide you with better protection. I suggest you head that way."

"How will we get there?" Virginia countered.

Mrs. Jamison wrung her hands, biting her bottom lip.

Charles understood her predicament and was sorry they had brought it into her home.

"I will let my husband know what has happened, and he will take you there. But I can't offer any more than that."

"How..." Virginia began.

"Thank you for your hospitality thus far and for your further assistance," Charles spoke up, cutting off her further pleas. Yes, this left them in an unappealing position, but the Jamisons had already given them so much and to ask for more would be selfish. "We understand the danger we have brought into your lives, and we apologize for it," Charles humbly replied.

Mrs. Jamison sighed, her body relaxing, grateful Charles didn't argue with her decision.

"We will be packed and ready to go by nightfall."

"Thank you. I will inform my husband." Mrs. Jamison turned and walked back out of the room.

"What did I tell you on the train?" Charles roared, rounding on Richard. He pointed an accusing finger in the other man's direction. "No more secrets! No more lies."

"I'm sorry," Richard said. "As I told you on the train, I am a selfish man who would do anything for Rose. I needed to ensure her safety, by any means necessary. If Mr. McPhearson ever found us, I needed to have a way to strike fear into his heart."

"Fear? All you have managed to do is anger him and gave him more reason to hunt us down. I told you if you ever endangered my wife again, we would be parting ways. You both can travel to Shiloh on your own. Virginia, Anna, and I will be on the first train leaving from Memphis."

"No!" Virginia shouted, rising to her feet and coming to stand in front of Charles. Hands on her hips, she glared up at him. "We will not abandon them. We started this trip together and will finish it as such."

"Richard's lies have endangered us all. He was warned what..."

"Yes, he was warned. And, yes, he lied, again," Virginia said, throwing a heated glance over her shoulder at Richard. "But he is a man in love. I understand why he did it. He needed to ensure that Rose's freedom would always be secure, and he needed to ensure that we would help him free her. Would you have still helped him if he had told you the truth?"

Charles recoiled from Virginia's accusation. How little did she think of him? Did she truly believe he would shrink away from helping someone obtain their freedom because of fear for his own safety? The journey thus far had proven otherwise. "Yes! Yes, I would have still helped him. I don't care about the ledger. I care that he lied about it. If he had told me the truth, I would have been able to create a better plan for these situations."

Virginia floundered formulating her response. She hadn't expected him to so vehemently defend his willingness to help.

Some of the steam deflated from the righteous indignation fueling her impassioned argument. She dropped her hands from her hips, removing the defensive edge from her posture. "You're right," she said in a softer voice. "We could have been able to plan better. But, again, we cannot abandon them. They need our help, and I, for one, will not turn my back on them. If you choose to leave, I shall not stop you, but know that you do it alone."

Charles ran a frustrated hand through his hair. He glared at Virginia making an attempt to intimidate her, but she met his stare without wavering. "Why must you be so stubborn, woman?" he growled.

Virginia gave him a triumphant smirk. "Because this is greater than us. Because I want my life to be about more than just me. I want to help. I won't stop serving those who need me."

Charles released a frustrated growl as he clenched and flexed his fingers repeatedly. The urge to punch or break something coursed through his body. He turned away from Virginia, closing his eyes and taking deep breaths to calm himself. "Alright," he said as he turned back around. "We will continue to help you," he said to Richard. "This is the last time I'll ask you, is there anything else you need to tell me?"

"No," Richard replied. "That is all."

"I will take you at your word, but know that if you break it again, my wife will not be able to talk me out of parting ways with you. And she will not be assisting you any further either. Understood?" Charles asked, casting his firm gaze at Virginia.

She crossed her arms over her chest and glared back, eyes

narrowed at him, but did not argue further.

"I understand," Richard replied humbly. "Again, thank you."

Charles didn't reply. Turning on his heels, he walked out of the room and headed toward the cellar for a moment of quiet to collect himself.

"We will head to Shiloh as Mrs. Jamison suggested," Charles threw over his shoulder as he left the room. "Mr. McPhearson will not follow us so closely to a Union encampment. And if he does, they will provide protection when we get there." Without waiting for a reply, Charles exited the room, leaving everyone to stare at his retreating back.

Virginia walked down the stairs into the cellar. Charles had been down there for several hours. She found him seated on a crate, slumped over, his elbows resting on his knees. He was so lost in thought he didn't hear her approach.

"Charles," Virginia called out softly.

He turned his head slowly, eyes a little unfocused as if being woken from a dream. "Come, my love," he said as he beckoned her forward, holding out a hand to her.

Virginia did as he asked and walked into his open arms. When she stood between his open legs, his strong arms encircled her waist, pulling her closer so that he could rest his head on her stomach. He released a low moan as she stroked her fingers through his silky hair.

"Are you still angry with Richard?" Virginia asked.

"Furious," Charles replied, his grip tightening around her waist. He let out a resigned sigh. "But I would have done the same if I were him."

"I would have as well," Virginia agreed.

"I am more upset over the situation than specifically at him. This mission was dangerous from the beginning, but I had calculated and mitigated the risks. Now I'm unprepared to protect you to the best of my abilities."

"I can protect myself," Virginia quipped with a light-hearted giggle to lighten the mood.

"I have no doubt about that, my fierce wife. But I am your husband. The majority of that role entails protecting and providing for you."

Virginia shifted in his arms. She tried to pull back slightly, but Charles would not let her out of his hold. Why did he have to say such things? Treating their relationship as if it were a true marriage. Virginia softened her gaze. Her stomach began to quiver as she looked into Charles's eyes. "Our marriage is not real," she said, barely above a whisper.

Charles dropped his gaze from hers, letting his arms fall to his sides. Virginia took a step back increasing the space between them.

"You are correct. Thank you for reminding me."

"Charles, I..."

"No, you are correct. I assume it has gotten late," he stated, changing the subject.

Virginia winced. She wanted to say more. To explain, but what she would explain she didn't know. Her throat went dry, rendering her unable to speak. She nodded her head in response.

"Then I should go speak with Mr. Jamison. I'm sure he'll be ready to leave soon." Charles stood and walked away, leaving Virginia standing next to the crate he just vacated, staring after him.

She wrapped her arms around herself as a shiver coursed through her body. She already missed the warmth of his embrace. Virginia cursed herself and her untamed mouth for ruining what was supposed to be a moment of comfort for Charles. She dropped her head, a bitter smile on her lips. Why, just once, couldn't she know how to give an adequate response?

Chest tight, body heavy, Virginia forced herself to follow Charles back to their companions. An apology already forming in her mind. If only she knew how to deliver it.

Virginia took Charles's hand, accepting his assistance into the wagon. It had been nearly an hour since their conversation in the cellar, and she had yet to come up with an apology.

"Thank you," she said, meeting his gaze as she stepped into the wagon. She tried to convey everything she wanted to but couldn't say with her pleading eyes.

"You're welcome," Charles replied in a clipped tone before turning to help Anna into the wagon.

Head hung low, Virginia took her place next to Rose. Noticing her distress, Rose reached out a hand and gently rubbed up and down Virginia's back. Virginia gave her a watery smile in thanks for the comfort. She glanced down at Rose's hand resting protectively on her swollen belly. A pang of envy pierced her heart. What would it be like to have a child growing in her womb? To have Charles's child growing inside her? If she was honest with herself, a part of her was sad that she would not find out.

Charles was a good man. A wonderful man. She couldn't ask for a better husband. Only she didn't want a husband. Right? Shaking away the thoughts clouding her mind, Virginia fixed her gaze on her hands clasped in her lap.

"Is that everyone?" Mr. Jamison asked as he came around the wagon peering inside.

"Yes, sir," Charles replied.

"Good. We should be there in several hours. I suggest you guys close your eyes and try your best to rest. I heard it's not that bad there, but you are going to a military encampment. You need to keep your wits about you."

"Thank you, again, for sheltering us and taking us to our next destination," Richard said.

"My pleasure. I'm only doing what the Lord called me to do." Mr. Jamison tipped the brim of his hat, then closed the flap on the wagon before disappearing around the corner to climb into the driver's seat. Encased in darkness, everyone settled into their seats as he suggested, ready for the long ride.

Chapter Eighteen

AR. ONE WORD WITH so many meanings. To some, it is a symbol of power and honor. A way for them to defend those they love and all they hold dear against the enemy. Scars and lost limbs to them were badges of honor they gladly wear.

To others, it is senseless death. The loss of fathers, brothers, and sons to defeat an enemy they weren't even sure was truly an enemy. To them, it is the death of many so that a few could keep what they loved, while the majority lost everything they held in the same esteem.

Virginia pulled back the wagon's cover ever so slightly, peering out over the encampment as they pulled into it. Some men milled about in the early morning sun, while others laid in their tents sleeping.

Those that were awake took care of their morning hygiene routine, scraping the whiskers of their new beard growth with knives, guided by their reflection in small pieces of glass. Virginia tried not to stare at those who were in various stages of undress; although, some of them with their bare chests covered in youthful muscles built from years of farming were quite pleasing on the eyes.

What did Charles look like under his shirt? Did he have a smattering of curly blonde hair like some of these men? Were his muscles lean and defined? From the feel of his arms wrapped around her last night, she assumed that they were. Virginia smiled to herself. Her thoughts had taken a shift to the proactive side as of late. Pushing away thoughts of her husband, Virginia focused back on the scene before her.

Tents littered the area as far as the eye could see. There must have been hundreds of soldiers here. They wore expressions of varying degrees of weariness, fear, and sorrow painted across their faces. They have been fighting in this war for over a year. Seen a year's worth of bloodshed. Been chased by the uncertainty of whether or not they would make it home to their families.

Virginia's heart broke for them. Yes, the entire country was at war, however, it was easy to forget what that really looked like when one lived in the North. Here in the South is where the majority of the action happened. Where the battles were fought, and the men died.

Virginia released the cover, allowing it to fall back into place. She glanced at Charles's sleeping form, his head hanging and bobbing with each jostle of the carriage. Why was he so handsome? It made resisting him that much harder.

Giving in to her need for comfort, just this once, Virginia scooted over and burrowed into his side. His sleepy eyes fluttered open looking at her. He lifted his arm and wrapped it around her, pulling her closer as his eyes fluttered closed again. Virginia rested her head against his chest, basking in the moment. Only this once, would she take comfort from him. Only this once.

"Time to wake up. We're here." Charles opened his eyes as Mr. Jamison's booming voice cut through his sleep-addled brain. He glanced at Virginia, who was nestled at his side. She smiled at him before lifting her head from his chest and rose to exit the wagon. He already missed the feel of her beside him. An apology for his peevish behavior last night would need to be given soon.

The other members of their small party stretched as they pushed away the remnants of sleep that still had a hold on them.

Alighting from the wagon, Charles lifted his hand to block the sun's early morning rays from burning his eyes. As his eyes adjusted to the light, he noticed the tent a few feet in front of him. It was larger than the ones the soldiers occupied. It must be the officer tent.

"In there is where you will find the Captain," Mr. Jamison said, confirming his suspicions. "You can plead your case to him."

"Thank you," Charles replied, extending his hand.

Mr. Jamison accepted the offered hand, giving it a firm shake. "I wish you the best."

He tipped his hat to Charles one last time before walking around to the driver's seat of his wagon. Richard, Rose, and Anna said their goodbyes and gave their thanks as he passed.

Seconds later, the wagon pulled off leaving them standing in front of the large tent.

Soldiers passing by stared in curiosity at their odd group, but none stopped to speak.

"Well, I believe it is time to enter and greet our new hosts," Richard said with a sardonic smirk as he tipped his head toward the tent. Despite the smile, he held Rose close in his iron grip. His watchful eyes tracking every man that walked by.

"Yes, I do believe you are correct," Virginia replied as she walked forward, disappearing within the tent. Charles, Anna, Richard, and Rose followed behind her.

Inside the tent was a hive of activity. Soldiers moved about hauling supplies, cleaning weapons, and organizing paperwork. A small group of men stood hunched over a large sawbuck table with maps and papers sprawled over it. Those must be the officers.

Back straight, head held high, Charles marched up to them. "Excuse me, gentlemen," he said in an assertive tone.

The group of men turned and looked at Charles then the rest of the party. There were a few raised eyebrows, some heads tilted to the side, and arms crossed over chests as the men surveyed the intruders.

"I beg your pardon for the intrusion, but my name..."

"Virginia?" one of the officers said, cutting off Charles's speech.

Charles focused on the young officer. His blue eyes were opened wide as he stared at Virginia as if seeing a ghost. Virginia stepped forward, her expression equally shocked. They stood staring at each other; both so still, it looked as if they forgot to breathe.

"Alex?" With a radiant smile that lit up her whole face, Virginia ran forward launching herself into the man's open arms. He held her close as he spun around. Laughs filled with the joy of reunion with someone dear to your heart spilled from the both of them.

Charles's body stiffened as a low snarl rumbled in his throat. His hands clenched and unclenched at his side as he was overcome with the sudden urge to punch something. Who is this man to Virginia? Why did he feel he could take the liberty of hugging her so closely? And her smile. She had never given him such a radiant smile.

"Virginia," Charles said in a menacing tone. "Please introduce me to your friend."

Sparks of red flashed across Charles's vision when the other man dared to tighten his grip protectively on Virginia's shoulders. He then leveled a threatening scowl at Charles.

"Oh!" Virginia chirped, a rosy flush spreading up her neck and across her cheeks. She tried to take a step away, but the man held on to her, keeping her at his side.

"Charles, this is Alex. Alexander Cummings," she quickly corrected. "We've known each other for years. Alex, this is Charles..."

"Her husband," Charles cut in, a slight gloating in his voice. He stepped forward and extended his hand to Alex.

Alex clasped Charles's hand making a loud clapping noise. They each held on to the other man's hand longer than necessary, squeezing with all their might.

"Yes, well," Virginia murmured in a peevish voice. "As I said, Alex is a dear friend." She stressed the word *friend*. The two men released each other but stood silently glaring at the other.

"Well," one of the other officers interjected. "As amusing as this jealous standoff has been, I'm curious to know, what brings your group here?"

Virginia focused on the man who had spoken, a warm smile on her lips. "Yes, thank you for asking, sir. We have come seeking refuge. We have rescued our dear friend Rose and are ferrying her to freedom. However, her master has been relentlessly pursuing us. We need your protection for a few days and possibly an escort to Ohio. We should be able to travel safely on our own from there."

The officer scoffed. "My dear girl, we are at war. There are battles to be fought and won. We need our men on the battlefield not chauffeuring people around the country. We are not your personal protectors."

"I'll do it," Alex broke in.

"But, Captain..." The officer said, his eyebrows furrowed and indignation written over his face.

"No, Lieutenant," Alex cut him off. "This woman is family to me. Her friends are my friends, and her mission is my mission. If she needs my assistance, I will grant it to her. And it should only be a few days to and from Ohio. A week maximum. I won't be gone long. As first lieutenant, you will take up my mantle until I return. Is that clear?"

"Yes, Captain," the man said with a nod of his head. He cut his withering gaze to Virginia before turning his back on the group.

"Good. Now, if you'll excuse me," Alex said to the other men in the tent, "I need to see about helping them get settled in."

"Yes, Captain," the men said in unison.

Alex extended his arm in front of him, inviting Virginia to precede him out of the tent. The thick silence that had enveloped the area moments ago erupted into a loud buzz of noise as men resumed their tasks.

Charles estimated that by the end of the afternoon gossip about the runaway slave, her companions, and the captain standing up for them would have spread through the entire camp. And they say women love to gossip.

Chapter Nineteen

"Rose I believe it was. And..." Alex said, focusing his clear blue gaze on Anna.

"Anna," she beamed.

"Anna, yes. Rose and Anna, this will be your quarters during your stay." Alex gave a flourishing bow and his most charming grin as he held open the flap of their tent. "It's not much, but I hope you ladies will be comfortable."

"It's perfect," Anna crooned with a sweet smile.

Did she bat her eyelashes at Alex? Virginia nearly laughed aloud seeing Anna's deep blush and the girlish infatuation shining in her eyes as she looked at Alex. Anna's smile was so wide her cheeks must have burned with the effort. Alex had that effect on women. He was a handsome devil with his ocean blue eyes, wavy ink-black hair, and dimpled grin. Too bad his heart was already taken. Although, Soleil would probably be amused by and even sympathetic of Anna's captivation with Alex.

The smile slipped from Virginia's lips as the weight of the moment slammed into her. She fought the tears that threatened to well in her eyes. Soleil was missing this. She was missing the chance to be here with Alex. As many months had passed for Soleil, as they had for Virginia, since she'd last seen Alex. She would never get to look at him with love and adoration again.

Virginia wanted to reach out and hug Alex again. To share her sorrow with someone else who understood. And to provide comfort he probably desperately needed. He wore a smile on his face, but what guilt and sorrow lay beneath it?

"If the rest of you will follow me please." Alex's smile faltered when he met Virginia's gaze. She tried to hide the sadness with a smile, but he had already seen it. He saw the piece of Soleil that haunted her.

"Yes, lead the way," Virginia said with too much cheer. Her voice sounded false even to her own ears.

Charles looked between her and Alex, a frown pulling at the corners of his mouth. No doubt he was wondering what had transpired between them.

"This way," Alex said, his voice a little dimmer. He began walking forward but paused when Richard didn't follow them.

Richard lingered at the entrance of Rose's tent whispering in her ear. She was trying to shoo him away, but he refused to leave her side.

Alex walked up to Richard and leaned in to speak low in his ear. "Believe me, I know what you are feeling. In fact, I envy your ability to protect your woman. But you have to be careful or your protection could harm her. Sometimes, it is best to watch her from afar."

"I will never let anything happen to her," Richard said with conviction.

"I said those same words once. Now she's gone." Alex gave Richard a sad smile and patted his shoulder. "Your love is beautiful, but it is more dangerous to her than to you. Do not let your love be the reason she is harmed. Even here, some people do not agree with your union. Don't test the hatred in other men's heart. Do you understand?"

Richard stood still, back rigid as he silently thought about Alex's words. With a curt nod, he stepped away from Rose. Alex began walking once more to show them to their tent. Richard's gaze lingered on Rose a little longer, but he followed behind Alex.

Virginia and Charles followed behind them. Her heart hurt for both men. Why did some men think they have the right to dictate with whom someone else could find happiness?

"And this will be the quarters for the newlyweds," Alex said, stopping in front of another tent a little distance away from Rose's and Anna's.

"Oh, um..." Virginia started to say.

"Thank you, this will do just fine," Charles replied as he placed his hand on the small of Virginia's back gently pushing her inside the tent. Virginia turned her head to thank Alex, but Charles was right at her back crowding her space, pushing her into the tent before she had a chance to.

Virginia rounded on Charles, hands on her hips, a withering glare on her face as soon as they were both in the tent, with the flap closed behind them. "That was rather rude of you."

"You and Alex have history. You share a connection of some sort that makes you smile and glow for him. I don't like it. I am your husband."

Virginia's frown gave way to a smile. Charles stood before her, hands clasped behind his back, posture rigid, and a deep scowl on his reddened face. "Are you jealous, Husband?"

"Of course, I am," Charles snarled. "A man I've never met, who looks like he can make even a prude swoon with his good looks, is hugging my wife too close and a little too long. I do not like it."

Virginia hadn't thought she'd be the type of woman who enjoyed shows of jealousy. In fact, two months ago, she would have described men who displayed such behavior with words such as oaf, primitive, or uncouth. But watching Charles brood over his speculations about her and Alex gave her a naughty spark of joy deep in her heart. "You are right. Alex and I do share a past. What does it matter what that past includes?" Virginia asked saucily.

"It matters a lot to me, because the past has spilled into our future." Hurt coated Charles's tone.

Guilt and shame ate away at Virginia's joy of teasing Charles. "There is nothing of a romantic nature between Alex and I. I'm sorry for insinuating that there might be. Only friendship exists between us. Alex's heart belongs to Soleil. He loved her as strongly and as deeply as Richard loves Rose. And that love has not diminished even though she's gone."

Charles's body relaxed, and the tension eased from him. He walked up to Virginia and wrapped his arms around her, hugging her close to his body. "I'm sorry for my jealousy, and for my peevish behavior last night. Virginia, I don't know what is holding you back from accepting this relationship, but it is my wish that one day you will."

"I..." Virginia began, her eyes cast to the ground. She ran her hands down the skirt of her dress, unable to meet Charles's gaze. He deserved an explanation. Even if she wasn't ready to give it.

"No. I don't expect you to say anything." Charles took Virginia's hands in his. "But I will always be honest with you, and this is how I honestly feel."

Virginia's heart hammered in her chest. Yet again, Charles chipped away at the armor around her heart. Lost for words, Virginia reached beneath her collar and pulled out the locket Charles had given her. "I can't give you exactly what you seek right now, but I want you to know that you are important to me. I hope that can be enough for now."

Charles ran a finger over the locket. He lifted it and tucked it back in her collar. "It will have to be," he said with a contented smile.

A beat of silence passed between them before Charles broke it. "Well, I do not know if you share my sentiment, but I am famished. Should we go in search of food?"

"Yes," Virginia said with an unsteady smile.

"Excellent." Charles walked toward the entrance of the tent, then stopped suddenly. Meeting Virginia's bewildered gaze with his devastatingly charming grin, he said, "Before I forget. Don't worry, Wife, I will be a perfect gentleman at night. Unless you don't want me to be, of course."

Virginia's mouth opened and closed, her eyes wide as she

stared at Charles, unable to speak. Before she could think of a reply, he bent to kiss her cheek, then turned and walked out of the tent. Virginia stood in his wake, her heart fluttering.

The stubborn part of her held to the notion that their marriage was only temporary and indulging in acts of pleasure with Charles was a bad idea. But another, ever-growing part of her wondered what Charles would be like when the gentleman was gone and the husband passionately loving his wife was set free.

Fanning herself against the warm Tennessee morning and sudden surge in her body temperature, Virginia took a few calming breaths before exiting the tent behind Charles

Chapter Twenty

S TARS SHONE BRIGHTLY IN the onyx sky. Each one twinkled above unaware of its beauty and how it affected the lives of the humans it cast its light upon. Virginia sat, back against the trunk of a tree, arms resting on her knees as she stared up at the enchanting night sky.

There was no greater peace than this. To sit under the stars that numbered amounts too great to count and be reminded how small you are in the totality of the vast universe. As she sat lost in the beauty of the night, a soft rustling nearby caught her attention.

"There you are," Alex's warm voice called out to her. "I've been looking for you. We haven't had much chance to speak."

Virginia gave him her brightest smile as Alex took a seat next to her. "Yes. Well, my arrival this morning was unannounced. And you are a captain in an army that is currently at war. Your time is precious and accounted for. I hold no ill feelings if you find yourself unable to engage in idle chatter with me."

"Yes, I am a captain, but that doesn't change the fact that you are a dear friend, and as such, it is my duty, when presented with the opportunity, to inquire how you fared in life since last we met."

Virginia's expression softened, touched by his words.

"After all," he continued, "the last time I saw you a husband was nowhere on the horizon. Now you seem to have captured one who is quite fond of you. What trickery did you use to make him blind to your rather unladylike qualities?"

Virginia laughed aloud. How she missed this. Good natured ribbing from old friends. "And what qualities would those be?" Virginia asked, quirking an eyebrow.

"Your inability to admit you are wrong. Your total disregard for social etiquette. Your constant need to voice your unsolicited opinion. To name a few."

"Ah, yes, those. Well, no tricks were needed. Only a simple compromise. My father would not allow me to participate in this endeavor to save Rose unless I was a married woman. I offered Charles some money in my inheritance, and he gladly accepted. The marriage will be annulled once we return to New York."

Alex snorted. "I would comment on the unromantic nature of that story, but I would expect nothing less from you. Although, I will say I don't know if I agree with your assessment of the situation. I think he is infatuated with you. Men do not puff out their chests in fits of jealousy for women they care nothing about."

"Yes, well, I..."

"You care for him, too. I can see it in your eyes."

"I do not," Virginia whined like a petulant child.

"You do. I think Charles is a good man. I spoke with him earlier today. Don't foolishly stand in the way of your own happiness. I would give anything to be able to..." Alex choked on the words. His voice raw with emotion, he finished, "To be able to hold Soleil one more time."

"I can't," Virginia said, barely above a whisper.

"But you can. You're the only one of us who can. If you'll excuse me, I need to go check on my men. I think I saw your husband near the chow tent playing cards. Go to him. Give what I wish I could give and receive what I wish I could receive." Alex stood and walked away.

Virginia sat for a little while longer repeating his words in her head over and over. Could she give in to her feelings for Charles? Should she? Still undecided, Virginia stood and went in search of the others.

⚯

"I see your nickel, and I raise you a quarter." Charles looked over his cards at the soldier across from him. They were the only two left in the poker game. Everyone else had bet all they were willing to lose.

The soldier looked at his cards then at the cards lined up in a row between him and Charles. A confident smile inched across his lips the longer he looked at the cards. He leaned back in his chair every bit a man brimming with confidence in his ability to win.

Those who decided to stay sat around them not speaking a word. Their eyes shined with the need to know who would win the pot. Who would take home their hard-earned money?

"All in." The soldier slapped the rest of his money on the wooden crate between them.

Charles didn't even look at the cards in his hands. He kept his stony gaze trained on the man before him.

"All in," Charles replied, placing his money on top of the pile.

The confident smile fell from the soldier's face. His eyes darted between the cards in his hand and the ones on display. His knee began to shake as he tapped his fingers on his thigh.

"Well?" Charles prompted.

The soldier wiped his arm across his forehead before placing his cards face up on the crate. Some of the men watching leaned in for a better look. He had a Full House. Not bad.

Charles showed his hand and was rewarded with a round of oohs and ahhs from the men. Straight Flush.

All the color drained from the soldier's face. He slumped back in his chair, defeated. No doubt he had bet more than he had to lose.

"Excellent game," Charles said, collecting the money from the crate. He did feel sorry for the soldier on some level, but for the most part, he saw this as a lesson in self-control for the young man.

"What's all this?"

Charles froze like a child caught with their hand in the sugar jar as the chiding female voice washed over him. He glanced over his shoulder to see Virginia striding toward him, hands on her hips.

"Hello, Wife," he said sheepishly. "We were playing a friendly game of cards."

"If it was as friendly as you say, why does his face look so sour?" Virginia stopped in front of Charles, eyebrow raised as she glared down on him.

He gave her his most charming smile, but it did nothing to erase her glowering expression.

The soldier perked up, seeing his saving grace in the fiery haired woman. "Because he won all my money, ma'am. Now I don't have anything to send home to my family." He cast his eyes to the ground, head bowed, hands folded in his lap.

Charles shot him a menacing scowl. How dare this puny little man try to use his wife against him? He lost fair and square.

Virginia gasped, placing her hand on her chest. "Charles, how could you take the money for his family? Give it back this instant."

"No," Charles grumbled. He shoved the money into his pocket to emphasize his point. He stood, shooting a pointed look at the soldier. "Maybe now he's learned his lesson about indulging in certain vices. And never to gamble with more than he is willing to lose."

"He is a soldier, risking his life to fight in this war. How could you even think about taking anything from him?"

Charles opened his mouth to respond, then snapped it shut thinking better of it. The wheels in his mind turned. This is an opportunity he might not have again. "If I give him his money back, you must compensate me for my loss."

"I don't..."

"Not with money." He stepped toward Virginia, crowding her space. "With your time," he said, his voice a silky caress.

Virginia leaned backward trying to restore the distance between them. Charles pressed further into her space. She swallowed hard. There was no place for her to go. A red flush crept up her neck.

Charles knew they were creating a spectacle for the soldiers sitting with their eyes glued to their every movement. It was probably the most exciting thing they had seen while sitting around in camp for some time.

"Alright," Virginia acquiesced. She lifted her hands up, pressing them to Charles's chest to push him back. At first, he didn't move. He stayed in her space, soaking in how flustered he made her.

"Good." Charles leaned back to give her the space she desired. He pulled the money out of his pocket, removing the little bit that belonged to him and placing the rest back on the crate. Looking around at the soldiers who remained, he said, "Take what is yours and help the rest find its way back to its original owners."

Then men pounced on the pile of money. Would the men who were not present receive their money back? Probably not. A squabble or two might even break out over it once the news of what Charles had done spread through the camp. But that was not his concern.

Charles extended his winged arm to Virginia. She accepted it and, to his surprise, snuggled close to his side. Charles smiled to himself. Gambling had never been this rewarding before.

Chapter Twenty-One

HANDS CLAPPED, FEET STOMPED, and men sang with the revelry of those who'd drank the cares of the world away.

I look over yonder and what a sight,
A buxom girl with eyes so bright.
From afar, she looks so good
Carry her off I think I should.
Sun has set, shadows come,
Time has fled, I'll take her to my bed.

Virginia bent low, dancing under the bridge of arms, as she clapped to the beat of the song. Charles followed close on her heels. He grabbed her in his arms and pulled her flush against his chest as soon as they came up. Virginia laughed with abandon as he spun them around, kicking up dust and dirt as they danced.

"I must say, Husband, dancing with you is one my new greatest joys." Virginia's smile stretched wide as she stared up into Charles's face as if he were a wonder to behold.

"Mine, as well. I dare say, you have ruined me for any other woman." Charles swept a stray curl that fell from her bun behind her ear.

The smile fell from her face, flattening into a thin white line as her sluggish brain processed his words. "Women want to dance with you? They come deal with me, the lot of them, if they think they are going to get a chance to dance with you." Virginia swept her hand in front of his face, swatting at the imaginary other women she currently loathed. She teetered a bit on her feet, making her movement so uncoordinated she barely missed slapping him.

She was so adorable in her anger. Charles smiled down at his inebriated wife. Maybe the second glass of whiskey wasn't the best idea. Nor the first, for that matter. Although, he was enjoying how talkative and free with her feelings it had made her.

Charles slowed their pace until they were no longer dancing to the beat. They simply swayed in each other's arms. He moved them to the edge of the crowd of men, making it a little easier to hear. "So, you want to keep me all to yourself?"

Virginia's eyes narrowed as she squinted up at him, shaking her head in confusion. "Of course. You're my husband. I have never been one to share what is mine."

Charles's chest rumbled with laughter. If a little bit of alcohol is what it took to get his wife to open up, he wished he'd given her some sooner. "Then why have you fought me so hard until now?"

Virginia stopped moving.

She didn't pull away, however, so Charles stood with her

in his arms waiting for her to find her words. The drunken fog cleared from her eyes enough for her deep buried pain to show through.

"Because I don't deserve to have love. Soleil loved Alex with everything in her. I selfishly only wanted to ever be free to pursue my own pleasures. Now she's gone. Snatched away from the only thing, the only man she ever wanted. Who am I to enjoy something I scoffed at when the person who deserves it the most will never be able to have it?"

Everything around them faded into the darkness as Virginia's words tore through Charles's soul. The hot pain that sliced through his chest nearly bought him to his knees. What must it feel like to carry that guilt? "I'm so sorry, Virginia," Charles said with a sad grimace.

"I never thought I would find love before I met you," she continued as if he hadn't spoken. She stared unfocused over his shoulder. "Then you came and made me want things that tear me up inside for wanting them."

Charles wrapped his arms around Virginia, hugging her tight. He tried to pass all the comfort and support from his body into hers through the embrace. "Virginia, what happened to Soleil was not your fault."

"I know. But..."

"No, buts. You can have love, Virginia. In fact, you owe it to her to try. Live the life she would have wanted for you and for herself. If what you say is true, Soleil would have given anything to live in a world where she and Alex could freely love each other. Do not take for granted what a gift it is that you have that chance."

Virginia stood silently in Charles's arms. She took a step back, creating an emotional chasm between them. Charles wanted to pull her back in close but didn't want to push her too far. Her unfocused gaze stayed trained on his chest. Charles said nothing. Did nothing. Only waited for her to make the next move.

They stood there silently for so long Charles wondered if the alcohol had addled her brain too much, inhibiting her ability to process this emotionally charged situation. Charles dropped his hands to his sides, accepting that Virginia wouldn't be giving him a reply. As he opened his mouth to suggest that they retire to their tent for the evening, Virginia reanimated, wrapping her arms around his neck and pulling him down until his lips crashed on hers.

It took a minute for Charles's brain to catch up with the situation, but when it did, he placed his hands on her hips pulling her body flush against his. Their tongues danced together as their mouths gave and took passion, longing, and unspoken hopes for the future. Burning desire worked through Charles's body, setting him on fire. This was it. Virginia, his wife, was finally giving herself fully to him. But she was under the influence of alcohol.

That thought sent an icy chill through his body, effectively killing the desire that burned through him moments ago. Pulling his lips from hers, he took a step back holding her at arm's length. "Stop. We must stop," he said in a husky voice tinted with unsatisfied desire.

"What?" Virginia asked groggily, as if being ripped from a most pleasant dream.

"We must stop," Charles repeated. "The day you give yourself to me fully, I want there to be nothing standing in the way. No reason that which you can call upon in the morning to claim our union was a mistake. I want you, Wife, but I want all of you, mind, body, and soul."

Virginia stared back at Charles bewildered. Her mouth hung open, but no words came out.

"Well," Charles said. "I will escort you back to the tent so that you can rest for the evening. I will leave you there alone for a while and rejoin the men until I can trust myself to honor the mandate I've just given."

Virginia nodded her head in understanding and allowed Charles to move her body so that she once again held his arm. He walked with her to their tent, then stood outside as she went in. Virginia looked over her shoulder one last time before disappearing between the tent flaps. It took everything in him not to go in after her. But as much as he wanted her, Charles wanted her even more the right way. And, thus, he would wait. Turning on his heels, Charles went in search of a distraction, leaving behind the tent and the alluring woman in it.

Chapter Twenty-Two

T HE EARLY MORNING SUN rose high in the sky shining its light down on everyone below. Virginia cursed the blasted thing as she stepped out of her tent. She wanted to hiss like a creature of the night as the bright light burned her eyes.

Squinting and holding her hand above her eyes, she maneuvered her head to find an angle where the sun could do the least damage. It was bad enough that the mirror had shown that she had red-rimmed puffy eyes. Never again would she accept a drinking challenge from her husband. The fiendish devil.

Apparently, alcohol did not have the same effect on him. He'd come into the tent sometime after she'd fallen asleep and was up and out of it before she awoke. If her rolling stomach decided to give in to the need to empty its contents, she would make sure her mouth was trained on his boots when it did.

Shuffling at a snail's pace, Virginia scuttled toward the chow tent. Once there, she found the rest of her traveling party chatting away, unhindered by any physical ailments. She loathed the whole lot of them. They all sat at a small table devouring their breakfast porridge and meat. As soon as Virginia neared, the food's aroma hit her nose, sending her stomach into an active rebellion.

"You don't look so well, dear," Anna chimed in, head cocked to the side as she assessed Virginia with concern. "You look a bit pale and green in the gills."

Charles, the evil man that he was, dipped his head, trying to hide his smile behind a spoon full of porridge.

"I assume I do. I feel as if little men are stomping through my skull. Not to mention the lovely feeling that my stomach wants to empty itself despite having nothing in it."

Richard and Charles erupted in laughter, earning glares from the women.

"Richard," Rose snapped. "How could you laugh at her in this state? And you," she said, rounding on Charles. "She is your wife and in pain. She needs you to comfort her not mock her."

Both men had the decency to cast their eyes to the ground, repentant pouts on their faces. Even if a hint of amusement still underlined it.

"Apologies, Wife," Charles said, standing up and walking toward Virginia. He leaned down and planted a kiss on her cheek.

Virginia gasped. The small contact seared her skin, sending waves of heat, more intense than usual, throughout her body. Her heart hammered in her chest as she found herself wanting to lean in and shift her head until their lips met. It was as if her body remembered something her mind couldn't.

She paused a moment to assess the current state of her body. The aches and pain seemed to be confined mostly to her head. A heavy sluggishness weighed down her limbs, but nothing seemed to be hurting in her delicate region. Virginia released a relieved breath. She walked on wobbly legs to the chair Charles had vacated and sagged into it.

Charles retrieved an empty chair and pulled it next to her and sat. He leaned toward her and whispered so only she could hear. "Don't worry. I was a perfect gentleman last night," he paused, his voice going lower, "although, you wished I wasn't."

Virginia's eyes widened, but she refused to turn and meet his gaze. A hot blush crept up her neck, engulfing her face.

"Well, you look horrid," Alex announced as he strolled up to their table, gaze trained on Virginia.

"This topic has already been discussed in its entirety and doesn't need your input. But I thank you for your most un-flattering assessment of me."

"Stay away from the bottle, and I will have nothing to assess."

All three men laughed as Virginia swatted at Alex. He jumped back, causing her to miss. Finding a chair of his own, Alex brought it over to and joined the small group. "I have news to report," he said to the group. "Mr. McPhearson is still on your trail. I estimate in about a day or so he may be able to track you all here. My men have been instructed to deny having seen you if that occurs, however, I think it best if we move soon. I have selected the party that will accompany us, and I am confident we can get you to Ohio safely."

"Excellent," Richard exclaimed. He leaned back to look

around Anna who sat between him and Rose.

"Rose, lo…" He caught himself, stopping the pet name from slipping past his lips. His eyes darted to Alex, then back to Rose. The corner of his lips pulled down in a slight frown. Remembering Alex's words of warning was probably hard and bothersome to him. Soon, the need for such precautions would be over. "Rose, how are you feeling? Are you up for travel?"

She smiled sweetly back at him. Excitement shone in her eyes. The time drew near when she could rest assured knowing she was free. "This baby is getting heavier each second, but I feel well enough to travel."

"Then we leave in two days," Alex said, hitting his hand against the table like a judge lowering their gavel after reaching a decision.

Virginia's face lit up with a radiant smile, despite her current ailing state. The excitement of being so close to the end of their journey overflowed from her heart. She reached out and took Charles's hand in her own, giving it a gentle squeeze. He had made this possible for her. He helped her take part, even in a small way, in this endeavor that meant so much to her. She would be forever grateful to him. "Charles, I…" Virginia snapped her mouth shut to listen to the rumbling in the distance. It grew louder, coming closer.

The men rose from the table heading to the tent's exit. As soon as they peered through the open flap, they immediately turned and ran back to the table. Each man grabbed one of the women, yanking them to their feet.

"We have to leave now!" Alex barked. His face had paled,

and his lips flattened into a thin white line. A focused, hawk-like alertness took over his features.

Each of the men wore matching expressions of determination, tinted with fear. Something was terribly wrong.

"What is happening?" Virginia asked as Charles dragged her from the table. He didn't respond, but she didn't have to wait long to receive the answer to her question.

As soon as they exited the tent, she saw the source of their panic. Hundreds of men in gray uniforms poured from between the trees, guns drawn. Confederate soldiers charged into the camp ready to do battle with the unsuspecting Union soldiers.

Their war cry and the stomping of their boots against the hard earth grew into a loud thundering chorus of impending death and destruction. Union soldiers scrambled to retrieve their weapons. Some had hands that shook so badly more bullets fell from their fingers than made it into their guns as they fumbled to load them.

As soon as the first wave of Confederate soldiers were within range, they opened fire. Charles pushed Virginia to the ground as bullets flew through the air. The urge to get up and run clawed at her until it became a physical need, but Charles's hand on her back kept her pinned to the ground.

"Stay low and follow me," Alex shouted over the commotion.

They got to their feet but squatted down low as they shuffled forward. Charles kept his hand locked around her wrist in a vise grip. Virginia continued to stumble as he half dragged her forward, faster than her rebelling body wished to move.

The pounding in Virginia's head doubled, making it hard for her to concentrate and stay coordinated.

She didn't know where they were going, but Virginia willed her body to keep moving. A shrill shriek spilled from her lips when a bullet flew past her ear, striking a soldier in the chest. The young man fell dead at her feet, his unseeing eyes staring at the sky as blood oozed from his wound. Virginia stumbled backwards, yanking her arm, until Charles lost his hold and she fell to the ground. She tried to scuttle backwards, but Charles soon grabbed hold of her again trying to yank her back to her feet.

"Come. We must keep moving forward," Charles commanded.

"No! No! No!" Virginia screeched as she continued to fight him.

"Snap out of it!" he barked. "Every second you waste is putting everyone in danger. Take a deep breath and start moving."

Virginia did as he commanded and pulled a large gulp of air into her lungs. Her heart continued its rapid pounding against her chest, but the fog of hysteria began to ebb away from her mind. She looked around and saw Alex holding on to Anna and Richard holding on to Rose in front of them, bent low, paused in their escape as they waited for her and Charles to follow. Everyone wore expressions of varying degrees of panic and fear.

Charles was right. She needed to stay focused and keep moving. She took another deep breath, then grabbed hold of Charles's hand. Everyone started walking again.

They continued on until they reached a tent that soldiers filed in and out of, retrieving weapons. Virginia was nearly knocked over by a soldier who rushed past, slamming into her as he entered the tent. Charles glared at the man, but now was not the time or place to address such slights.

"Take one of each," Alex said, handing a pistol, a rifle, cartridge box, and cap box of ammunition to Richard and Charles. "Do either of you ladies know how to shoot?"

They all shook their heads no. That is the one unladylike pursuit Virginia's father absolutely refused to allow her to partake in. He called it dangerous and unnecessary, as a woman would never have reason to fire a weapon. She cursed herself for not fighting him harder on that point.

"Carry these and use this to protect yourself if needed." Alex handed each of them several cartridge boxes and cap boxes. He also gave them a saber, showing them how to properly grip it as he placed it in their hands.

"Let's move," Alex commanded once they were all loaded down with weaponry. They left the tent and again bent low to move to a destination Virginia didn't know.

Soldiers from both sides were now everywhere fighting each other to the death. Guns fired, swords clashed as the carnage of battle raged. Screams echoed through the air. Blood painted the earth in its warm, russet stain. Men who had never seen each other before and held no personal qualms sent each other into the awaiting arms of death. Ripping each other from family and friends.

Tears ran unchecked down Virginia's face. Her heart ached for every one of the men here today. They condemned each other to an irrevocable death, and for what? Country, money, power, land, pride? Things that in the grand scheme of life are unworthy of the sacrifice of never being able to hold their baby, kiss their wife, or laugh and cry ever again. Virginia sent up a silent prayer as she ran through the fighting men, that someday soon, peace would be restored.

Alex led them to a corral of horses. The animals whined and galloped around the small area, agitated by the shouting and gunfire. Alex, Richard, and Charles ran into the corral, each grabbing the reins of a horse.

Richard hoisted Rose on a horse and swung up behind her. Charles did the same with Virginia. Alex helped Anna onto the third horse but did not climb on after her.

"Do you know how to ride?" Alex asked Anna. She nodded her head in confirmation. "Good." He took a step back from the horse and turned his attention to Charles. "Head north. Ride at a hard gallop and don't stop until the horses are ready to give out."

"Be safe," Charles replied.

"Wait," Virginia called out to Alex. "Aren't you coming with us?"

"No. I need to fight next to my men."

"But you may die," Virginia shrieked on the brink of hysteria.

Alex didn't respond. He gave Virginia a sad smile as he took a few more backward steps away from the horses. Charles snapped the reins of their horse, spurring it into motion.

"No!" Virginia wailed. She twisted in the saddle trying to fling herself to the ground. Charles's iron grip kept her in place despite how hard she fought. The horse galloped away leaving Alex to watch them escape. Virginia looked over her shoulder, hot tears streaming down her face, until Alex was swallowed by the trees.

Charles, Anna, and Richard pushed the horses to run as fast as they could. Their hooves beat against the ground with each powerful stride. Tree branches and other foliage occasionally struck them as they careened through the woods at a dangerous speed.

They moved so quickly they didn't see the soldiers until it was too late. A group of Confederate soldiers lied in wait, unseen on the ground, muskets aimed and ready to fire. As soon as the horses were within range, they opened fire. Charles threw himself over Virginia to cover her body with his. They leaned low over the side of the horse for cover.

Bullets rang out from multiple directions, but Charles kept the horse moving forward. Charles and Richard returned fire, hitting some of the soldiers.

A high-pitched feminine cry reverberated through the air. Virginia tried to look at the other riders, but Charles's heavy body on top of hers made it impossible for her to move.

The horses continued running, moving them past the ambush. Even once the shooting stopped, Richard and Charles kept the horses moving. Soft cries mixed with the heavy hoof beats.

"We need to find shelter soon. Rose has been hit," Richard called out.

"We'll stop at the first home we come to. We will pay them to take us in if we must," Charles replied.

The small group continued to ride for what seemed like hours, until they finally saw a small wooden cabin in a clearing in the distance. They guided the horses toward it, each hoping and praying the owners wouldn't be hostile.

As they approached, an older couple stepped onto the porch of the cabin, the man holding a rifle in his right hand. He didn't aim it at them, which was a good thing. They pulled the horses to an abrupt stop in front of the cabin.

Richard hopped from the horse and pulled a moaning Rose from the saddle. He cradled her in his arms like a delicate piece of porcelain as he ran toward the front steps. "Please, she's been shot. She's with child. We need your help," Richard pleaded.

"Bring her on in here," the man replied in a slow Southern drawl. "I'll fetch some hot water, while Ma takes a look at her."

"Thank you." Richard bounded up the steps and entered the cabin.

Charles helped Virginia from the saddle, then Anna from hers. Virginia's body shook like a delicate flower caught in the vicious winds of a thunderstorm. She wrapped her arms around herself, hugging her middle for comfort. The little that was in her stomach spewed from her mouth as her body violently shook with the effort of vomiting.

Anna walked up to her and held back her hair while she heaved. When she was done, Virginia wiped her mouth on her sleeve, uncaring if it was appropriate etiquette or not. Her chest heaved, and her limbs continued to shake as the fear and adrenaline coursed through her body.

No words were spoken by those left outside reeling from

what had just transpired. They each stood, locked in their own personal states of shock and disbelief. Needing comfort, Anna pulled Virginia close for a hug. Both women held on to each other, crying. Charles opened his arms wide and enveloped them both in his embrace. They stood like that, each giving and receiving comfort from the others, until Rose's loud cry exploded from the cabin. Releasing each other, they ran into the house to see what was happening.

Chapter Twenty-Three

EVERY PART OF VIRGINIA's body shook. Her hands that struggled to grasp the cloth tight enough to wring the warm water from it. And her legs, which could barely muster the strength to carry her across the room to Rose's bedside.

The tragedy of the day was too much. First, watching as the soldiers slaughtered each other. The large loss of lives, which could still be climbing at this very moment if the battle continued to rage on. Then, the possible loss of Alex if he were slain on the battlefield. And, now, Rose who writhed in pain on the small bed afraid for her child.

"Stay calm, my dear. Everything will be fine. We need to get this bullet out first, then we can worry about the baby." Mrs. Johnson, whose home they currently occupied, ran a soothing hand over Rose's hairline to try to keep her calm. She began to hum while she waited for Virginia to finish fixing the warm wet rags and Anna to return with her medical bag.

The bullet had struck her thigh, right below her hip. The small orb was still lodged in place in need of removal. Rose laid on the opposite side to keep pressure off the wound.

Rose's water had broken sometime during the ride to the cabin, adding to the complications. Mrs. Johnson had checked and estimated there would be enough time to remove the bullet before the baby came, but they would need to act quickly.

"Please, save my baby," Rose whimpered as tears ran down her dirt-stained cheeks. "Something's not right. I feel it. Save my baby."

"Your baby will be fine. We will meet him soon. But, first, we need to worry about mama first."

Anna rushed through the bedroom door medical bag in hand. Virginia wrung the last of the rags and brought it over to the pile on the small table next to Rose's bedside.

"Alright, girls, I'm going to need your help. Anna, I need you to hold her hand. This is going to be very painful. Whatever you do, make sure she stays on her side."

"Yes, ma'am," Anna said as she ran to the side of the bed and knelt before Rose. She took her hands into her own and assumed the mantle of comforting the fear reflected in Rose's eyes. Anna hummed her favorite hymn, "Amazing Grace," as she stroked a gentle hand over Rose's forehead.

"And, you. I need you to keep wiping the blood away as I dig out the bullet. I need to be able to see what I'm doing, so just keep wiping."

"Yes, ma'am," Virginia said as she grabbed the tray of warm rags from the bedside table, placing it in her lap when she sat on the bed behind Rose.

Mrs. Johnson dug through the bag and pulled out the tools she would need, which included a probe to dig out the bullet, suture thread and needle, bandages, and a bottle of whiskey.

She laid the items out neatly on the bed so she could have easy access to them.

She poured the whiskey over the needle and probe to sanitize them. Once she was ready, she gave Virginia and Anna a nod to signal it was time for their part to begin.

Anna clamped down even tighter on Rose's hands and increased the volume of her humming. Rose's agonizing scream split the air as Mrs. Johnson dug the probe into her wounded flesh. Virginia picked up a rag and, with shaky hands, wiped away the blood that oozed from the wound.

Mrs. Johnson leaned in and tilted her head to try to get a better visual of the bullet. She shifted the probe fractional amounts causing Rose to cry out repeatedly. "Look inside my bag and pull out the leather strap. Have her bite down on it," Mrs. Johnson instructed Anna.

She did as she was told and rummaged through the bag until she found the strap. Mrs. Johnson stopped moving the probe until Anna placed the strap in Rose's mouth.

"Bite down hard on that, dear, whenever you feel the pain," Mrs. Johnson commanded.

Rose gave a weak nod. Virginia used one of the rags to wipe the sweat and tears from Rose's face as she moaned and cried around the leather in her mouth.

Mrs. Johnson continued the procedure, moving the probe to find the bullet. Rose bucked and twitched occasionally, but Anna held her down reducing the movement. Mrs. Johnson dug around a little longer. "I think I found it." She twisted the probe one last time, clamped it around the bullet, and pulled it out.

Virginia placed a rag over the wound to staunch the blood flow. Her heart beat an erratic tempo in her chest. Each of Rose's cries of pain tore a new hole in her heart. She tried her best to keep her clammy hands away from Rose's warm skin so as not to add to her discomfort.

Mrs. Johnson used one of the rags to wipe the blood from her hands. "That's it, dear. The worst is over." She picked up the bottle of whiskey and peeled back the rag Virginia held over the wound and poured the amber liquid over it.

Rose released another muffled scream, her chest heaving up and down while her cheeks inflated and deflated rapidly as she inhaled and exhaled rapid breaths.

Mrs. Johnson threaded the needle, tied it off, then began to close the wound. It only took six stitches, and then it was over. "You did great. It's over now."

Mrs. Johnson placed a bandage over the wound and held it in place, while she and Anna rolled Rose onto her back. She wiped her hands clean again, then poured the whiskey over them. After drying them, she lifted the hem of Rose's chemise to check on the progress of her delivery.

"Looks like the baby is impatient to meet you. Rest for a little bit. We will get new rags and fresh hot water. You'll need to deliver the baby soon," Mrs. Johnson said as she rose from the bed then walked out of the room.

Virginia and Anna climbed in the bed each lying on either side of Rose. They cuddle close, careful not to aggravate her wound. Virginia grasped Anna's and Rose's hands, clutching them in hers.

"I don't know if you ladies would agree, but the end of the

day cannot come soon enough," Anna said.

Rose and Virginia chuckled.

"It would appear we need to welcome my child into the world first," Rose replied in a weary tone.

"You know, that is a perfect way to end the day. End it with love and goodness," Anna replied. "God knows the world needs it."

Chapter Twenty-Four

CHARLES SAT IN A rocker on the cabin's front porch next to Richard. Mrs. Johnson had come out several hours ago to inform them that she had removed the bullet from Rose's shoulder and sewn the wound shut. Overcome with joy, Richard had fallen to his knees weeping.

Charles's heart had frozen in his chest as he watched the other man. It had been a long time since he'd seen something that stirred his heart so much.

Now they waited for more news as the women delivered the baby. The anticipation was maddening. Mr. Johnson had suggested that they join him in tending his crops to keep their bodies and minds occupied, but they had declined. Charles now regretted that decision.

"Rose changed my life," Richard said in a voice soft with affection, breaking the silence between them. "I had no purpose before her. I squandered my wealth, chasing fleeting pleasures. I was empty. But Rose saw the mess that I was, and she loved me anyway. She loved me so well I wanted to be a better man for her. I wanted to give her the world, because she deserves nothing less."

Richard stared off, unseeing into the distance. Charles said nothing. He waited for Richard to find his words and continue to unburden his heart.

"When I saw the blood. When I thought I could lose her, I..." Richard choked on his words. He released a heavy breath to bring his emotions under control. "I don't know what I would do without her."

"You won't have to find out," Charles replied in a reassuring tone. "Her wound will heal. She'll deliver your child, and you will raise it together as you grow old together. Banish all thoughts of the contrary from your mind."

"You're right." Richard relaxed back into his chair and stared into the distance lost in thought. A companionable silence descended between them.

Charles understood Richard's fear. Heart stopping terror that you will be too late or not enough to protect the one you love from harm. Wanting to give up everything, even your own life, if it means they will be safe. Fear born of loving someone else more than yourself.

Watching as bullets flew past Virginia, missing her by mere inches, nearly drove Charles mad. He'd wanted to throw her to the ground and cover her with his body to absorb the bullets but knew that wouldn't truly keep her safe. His gratitude knew no bounds that she had been spared the pain of a physical battle wound. The emotional wounds, they would deal with together.

Charles's and Richard's heads snapped to attention at the sound of the cabin door creaking open. Mrs. Johnson walked onto the front porch, wiping her hands on a hand towel. She kept her eyes cast to the ground, not meeting their gazes. Silence stretched between them as Richard and Charles waited for her to deliver news of Rose and the baby.

"Ain't no easy way to say this, so I'll get to the point. Rose didn't make it. She bled out after the delivery."

The words exploded in Charles's chest, blowing his heart into tiny pieces. He couldn't move, couldn't speak, couldn't think. His head turned at a sluggish pace toward Richard. His eyebrows furrowed as he took in the other man. Richard was on his knees, head thrown back, mouth open as he howled his agony, but Charles heard nothing. It was as if all the sound had been sucked from the world. He shook his head, trying to clear it. And then it hit him.

Misery, grief, and heartache, given life in the cries of a man who would never be the same again. Richard roared his pain like a desperate hurting animal. Charles took it all in, trying to memorize every second of this moment because he knew it would haunt him until the day he died. In the midst of the pain, a ray of light sliced through the darkness of Charles's mind. "The baby?" Charles asked.

"Babies," Mrs. Johnson corrected. "A boy and a girl. They are both healthy."

Charles gave thanks for the small miracle. Rising from his chair, he stepped in front of Richard and pulled him to his feet. "Did you hear her? You're a father now. You have two people who depend on you now. The last two parts of Rose. They need you to be strong now. To focus on them."

"I...I can't. Not right now." Richard jerked free of Charles's grasp and stormed down the steps.

Charles watched him go, heart breaking anew

Virginia sat on the riverbank staring at her reflection in the water. The movement of her feet as she swirled them in the water caused a ripple that distorted her features. It was fitting. A true reflection of her heart. Twisted and mangled to the point of being unrecognizable.

Another friend was lost. Another soul wrongfully separated from the ones they loved and who loved them back. When would it end? When would men no longer feel the need to harm and kill each other?

The sound of heavy footsteps coming closer reached Virginia's ears, but she did not turn to face the intruder. Finding words to comfort another person was a task she didn't have the energy to complete at the moment.

"There you are. I've been looking all over for you."

Charles's smooth rich voice glided over her like a calming balm on her aching heart. Virginia wanted to jump up and throw herself into his arms. To draw the comfort she so desperately needed from his warm embrace. But she stayed where she was, eyes glued to her reflection in the water. "Yes. Here I am," she replied in a flat dull tone.

Charles sat down next to Virginia, so close their shoulders brushed with each breath she took. She wanted to lay her head against his shoulder and sit quietly giving and receiving comfort. But her back remained rigid and she made no moves to act on her desires.

"How are you feeling?" Charles asked.

Virginia gave a humorless laugh. "How am I feeling? How is one supposed to feel after watching a friend die? Especially after watching that friend cheat death once and being given false hope, only to have it ripped away hours later."

Charles said nothing in reply. For that she was grateful. What could one say? What words could someone use that would have meaning in a time like this?

Charles reached out an arm to wrap around her shoulders and pull her close.

"No," Virginia said as she leaned away from his embrace. "Don't touch me."

"I only want to comfort you."

"I know. Which is why I don't want you to touch me. I don't want your comfort. I need to get through this on my own."

"Why? You're not in this alone. You don't feel this pain alone. Do you think I'm not devastated as well? I need to receive comfort from you just as much as I need to give it. Why are you denying us this?"

"Because the pain is too great."

Charles ran a frustrated hand through his hair. "I don't understand."

"I know. I'm sorry. Please leave me alone." Virginia pulled her feet out of the water and brought her knees up to her chest. She wrapped her arms around her legs, hugging herself tightly. All the while, she kept her eyes averted from Charles. Dismissing him.

"I don't understand you, Virginia. You continue to pull away from me, when all I want to do is give you love, comfort, and support. Here."

Charles reached into his pocket and pulled out a letter. Eyebrows furrowed, Virginia's questioning eyes looked from the letter to Charles. He said nothing as he held it out to her. Virginia took the letter from his hands and stared at it. Scrawled across the front in her father's bold handwriting were the words *To Charles and Virginia.*

"It is from your father. The letter he gave me on the day we wed. He wrote in it a section for you and told me to give it to you when I'd finally won your heart. But I don't think that shall ever be, so I give it to you now. I don't know what it says. I didn't read past what was meant for me, but may you find peace with his words." Charles stood from beside her and began to walk away.

Virginia watched him go wanting to call out to him. Wanting to unburden her heart and tell him all that plagued her. To shout, I do! I do love you! But she didn't. Her lips remained sealed, and the words both their hearts needed to hear remained locked inside.

Chapter Twenty-Five

EVEN IN THE EARLY morning light of a new day, the pain had not lessened, but it was tinted with the joy of possibility. Virginia stood next to Richard, staring at the small wooden box deep in the earth. Some might say that all that remained of Rose lay in that box. But Virginia knew better.

The last remnants of Rose lay sleeping in her and Richard's arms. She looked down into the angelic face of the little boy she held close and saw Rose clear as day. In his bow-shaped lips and round nose. One day, when he was older, Rose would appear in his character. In the way he loved and gave generously.

Richard named the children Roseline and Ashton. Ashton had many of Rose's features, but his father's pale cream skin and green eyes. Roseline was a beautiful mixture of them both with a light wheat complexion and honey eyes. Virginia could already tell her beauty would capture the attention and heart of many men. Richard would have his hands full keeping the suitors at bay.

They stood quietly as the pastor said a few words meant to give comfort to the living. Once he was done, Charles and Mr. Johnson picked up their shovels and began filling the hole with dirt. Virginia looked across the small hole, which could have been a canyon for all the hurt feelings and unspoken words between her and Charles. He hadn't spoken to her the remainder of last night or this morning. And she didn't blame him.

"Walk with me," Richard whispered to Virginia. He turned and began walking from the graveyard before Virginia could agree or deny his request. She followed behind him a few seconds later.

"He loves you. Charles," Richard said as soon as she came to his side.

"I know," Virginia replied on a whisper.

"And yet you shun him? Why?"

Virginia held Ashton tighter to her chest, pulling comfort from his small body. Facing a bullet was easier than facing her truth. She kissed his forehead, closed her eyes, and took a deep breath. "Because I'm afraid."

"Of love?"

"Of losing someone I love. The pain of losing friends has been crippling. Imagine the pain of losing the person who holds your heart. I don't think I would survive it."

"I don't have to imagine," Richard replied with a sad smile.

Virginia touched her hand to her chest, cursing herself for being so careless with her words. "I didn't mean..."

"I know." Richard gave her a reassuring smile. "I have never experienced a pain as bad as losing Rose. Without the children, I'm sure I would have died of a broken heart. But I would not trade one second of my time with Rose; even if it meant never having to feel this pain. The pain is a testament to how much I loved her and felt loved in return. It is because I experienced such intense joy with her that I now feel the crushing sorrow of her loss. Do not hide your heart away because of fear of pain. You will experience sorrow in life no matter what, at least allow yourself the courtesy of having joy to accompany it."

Richard was right. She could not control what happened in this life. Events both good and bad would happen whether she wanted them to or not. Blocking out the goodness and love because of the fear of the hurt that would come regardless was foolish. No longer would she allow fear to rule in her life.

"You're right." Virginia stopped walking and looked up at Richard. "I will tell Charles how I feel and beg for his forgiveness. Thank you, Richard. I truly hope you find happiness again."

"I will. Each day I look at my children and tell them stories of their wonderful mother, my soul will get to relive a moment of joy. The pain will lessen with each of those moments."

As Virginia looked into Richard's eyes, she believed him. Despite having every reason to be filled with bitterness, he wasn't. All she saw reflected in his gaze was understanding and acceptance.

"Come. Let us return to the cabin. The little ones need to eat."

Virginia's heart warmed even more at Richard's reminder. He truly was a wonderful man. He purchased a slave woman and her infant from a neighboring farm. He offered her the choice of freedom or to grant his request that she accompany him to England and act as wet nurse for the twins. He even offered her a generous salary and a home for her and her child in England. He was a good father and generous man.

Charles came to attention as his ears picked up the sound of the hoof beats of several riders in the distance. He stood from his rocker and walked to the edge of the porch as the small posse came into view. There were three men.

Dust and dirt were caked on their faces and clothing. Worn-out, mean expressions marred each man's face, telling the story of the long relentless journey they'd taken. Charles leaned against the railing waiting patiently for them to ride up to the front of the cabin.

"Good day, gentlemen," Charles said in an easy tone when they finally pulled their horses to a stop in front of the porch. "How may I help you today?"

One of the men, the oldest in the group, swung down from his horse and took a few commanding steps in front of the others. This must be Mr. McPhearson. He had a full head of salt and pepper hair, and despite his advanced years, his body remained well muscled and spoke to the fact that he kept himself active. His astute gaze stayed locked on Charles as he walked, like a hunter assessing its prey.

Charles found it odd that he'd personally come all this way to find Rose. Especially when he could have sent a bounty hunter after them and saved himself the trouble of a long ride on his old bones.

"My name is Henry McPhearson," the man said, confirming Charles's suspicions. "I own a plantation over in Memphis. One of my slaves, a young colored woman by the name of Rose, escaped a few days back. She's heavily pregnant. I think she had help from some white men. Abolitionist. I've been tracking them this way, and I was wondering if she'd passed through these parts?"

"Can't say I seem to recall anyone by that description," Charles lied.

Mr. McPhearson's eyes narrowed on Charles. "You own this piece of land?"

"No, sir. I'm a guest of the owners."

"Mind if I talk to them?"

"No need," Richard's booming voice called out as he and Virginia emerged from the side of the cabin. "Rose is dead. She died giving birth."

Mr. McPhearson's face crumbled at Richard's words. The color drained from his face, and his mouth flapped open and closed as if his brain couldn't produce the words he wanted to say. "You're lying," he said in a choked voice.

"I wish I were, but I'm not. Rose is gone."

Mr. McPhearson bent forward placing his hands on his knees as he struggled to take in short choppy breaths. His eyes watered, filling with tears until one escaped and ran down his wrinkled cheek.

Charles studied the man, confused. Mr. McPherson's actions were that of a man mourning someone he loved, not a man upset at losing a piece of property.

Taking a few deep breaths, Mr. McPherson calmed himself. He wiped away the tears from his eyes and stood facing Richard and Virginia. "Are those her babies?"

"Yes, sir," Richard respectfully replied.

Mr. McPherson took a step forward and stopped. "May I see them?"

Richard nodded, giving his consent.

Mr. McPhearson removed his hat from his head clutching it in front of him in a tight grip. He inched forward, stopping in front of Richard and Virginia, who held the sleeping babies in their arms. "They look just like her," Mr. McPherson said in a voice full of amazement and wonder. His awe gave way to determination as his jaw set in a hard line. "I want them back. They belong to me."

"My children belong to no one," Richard growled. He stepped in front of Virginia blocking Mr. McPhearson's view of Ashton and tightened his hold on Roseline.

"So, you're the father then. I don't care. Rose belonged to me, so those children belong to me."

"No! Only death will keep me from my children."

"Don't make it come to that, son. Just give them to me." Mr. McPherson placed a hand on the gun in the holster at his waist. The two men on the horses behind him did the same.

"Why do you want them so badly?" Virginia asked, stepping from behind Richard.

"Rose is...was my daughter. Her mother, Mary, was the love of my life. She was all I had left of her. I kept Rose safe, gave her everything she ever needed. And then you come and take her away from me. Those babies are all I have left of Rose and Mary. I want them."

Virginia gasped, her eyes wide, and lips parted in shock over the new revelation.

Charles clenched his fists at his side, but quickly released them. Yet another secret Richard kept from them. But in light of the current situation, it didn't matter.

"No," Richard firmly stated. "These children are mine, and they will stay with me. I know you are hurting. I feel the same pain, but it is time for you to let go. You didn't protect Rose; you locked her away, treated her like an object to be collected and preserved. You didn't allow her to live and experience the life that she wanted to live."

"I did it for her!" Mr. McPhearson bellowed, slapping his hat against his thigh.

"You did it for yourself!" Richard roared back. "You did it so that you could hold on to a piece of your own happiness. So that you could ignore the pain of losing Mary. I didn't have to force Rose to leave with me. She wanted to. She wanted to be free of being under your thumb."

Mr. McPhearson stumbled backwards as if Richard had dealt him a physical blow. All his anger deflated. "I only... I..."

"I know," Richard said in an understanding tone. He reached out and placed a hand on the older man's shoulder. "Letting go is hard, but if you truly love them, you will. What kind of life can they have here in the American south? With me, they will want for nothing, and they will be raised with all the dignity and respect due them."

"What do you mean?"

"My Christian name is Richard, but in England, my title is Earl of Devon. My children will be afforded all the privileges of my title."

A thick silence fell over everyone present as the weight of Richard's statement settled between them.

Charles had a new respect for him. Bringing a woman of African descent home with him to England was already a bold decision. Doing so when you were of the English peerage was astounding. Charles let out a bark of laughter. "You, my friend, are a crazy devil."

Richard gave him a cocky grin. "I have never been one to be able to deny myself what I wanted. No matter the cost."

A tentative smile slowly grew over Mr. McPhearson's lips. Patting Richard on the shoulder, he said, "Take them. Love them and give them everything I wish I could. The only thing I ask is that you let me accompany you to New York. I want to spend some time with them before I never see them again."

"You are always welcome to visit us in England."

"Nah. I'm an old Southern farmer. I ain't meant to be on a boat sailing across the ocean. You just keep them safe."

"I will."

Richard extended his hand to Mr. McPhearson. He accepted it with a firm grip; his hard eyes boring into Richard's. The two men came to a silent understanding. The mantle of protector was being passed from one to the other. A role in which failure could not be accepted.

As they released each other's hands, Anna and Mrs. Johnson came around the corner of the cabin from the direction of the garden, each carrying a basket of vegetables. Their chatter ceased when they noticed the newcomers.

"Oh, hello. Who are these gentlemen? Did I miss something?" Anna inquired. Everyone erupted in laughter.

"Yes, my dear. You missed quite a lot," Virginia said with a warm smile. "Come, let us go prepare something to eat for our new guest; if that is alright with you, Mrs. Johnson. I'm sure they are famished."

"Fine by me."

"Yes, ma'am, we are. We thank you kindly," Mr. McPhearson said

Charles sat back in his rocker as the women passed by to enter the cabin. Virginia paused and looked at him briefly as if she wanted to say something, then cast her eyes away and entered the house. He would address the rift between them later when they could be alone. For now, he watched Richard and Mr. McPhearson talk with fond remembrance of Rose. Each day of this trip seemed to be filled with more and more surprising events.

Chapter Twenty-Six

RINKS FLOWED, FOOD WAS consumed, and all-around merriment was had by everyone. Virginia smiled as she looked around the room. Charles, Anna, Richard, Mr. McPhearson, and his three men sat around the table, enjoying their final meal together in Tennessee.

Virginia basked in the moment. Differences were set aside, forgiveness had been given and received. And now they laughed and broke bread together. Moments such as this were so rare in life, but that is what made them so precious.

They dined in the restaurant of their hotel on a meager meal of stew and warm fresh bread, but it could have been the mightiest of feasts for all the satisfaction that was had by all in attendance.

Earlier that morning, they had left the Johnsons' cabin with abundant words of thanks and well wishes. They arrived back in Memphis a few hours ago. In the morning, Mr. McPhearson's men would return to his plantation, while the rest of their group would begin their return journey to New York.

The clinking of a fork against a glass captured everyone's attention, sending a hushed silence over the room. Richard pushed back his chair and stood holding his glass in the air.

"I hope you all do not mind, but I wanted to say a few words." Everyone nodded their heads in encouragement. "This trip will be one I never forget. I lost the love of my life, mother of my children. A hole has been blown through my heart that will never be filled again. But I have also found new friends and mended broken ties. Which reminds me..." Richard reached into the pocket of his frock coat and pulled out a small black ledger book. Handing it to Mr. McPhearson, he said, "I believe this belongs to you."

"Thank you, son." Mr. McPhearson accepted the offered book and tucked it in his pocket.

"Thank you, Charles, Virginia, and Anna, for joining me on my heart's mission. I have grown both as a man and as a human being because of it. I want you all to know that you each have changed my life forever, and I will never be able to thank you enough. To good friends!"

"To good friends!" Everyone chorused, raising their glasses.

Virginia looked across the table at Charles. His dazzling smile illuminated his face, giving it a radiant glow. He was it. Her husband, her partner, and her friend.

A warm blush crept across Virginia's cheeks when he looked up meeting her gaze over the table. He blinked several times, then his face softened, his smile trained on her. "How are you faring tonight, Wife?"

"Well; although, I've recently realized I miss my husband."

Charles's eyes widened slightly, a spark of desire coming to life in their depths. Her words were simple, but their meaning was great, and he understood. "He has been in the same place, patiently waiting for you to come to him."

Virginia said nothing in return. She simply held his gaze, a flirtatious smile on her lips. Tonight was the night. Tonight, they would become one.

Virginia paced outside the hotel room door going over her plan yet again. She wrung her hands, then shook them to dispel her nervous energy. Why was this so hard? Because it would require her to be vulnerable, that's why. She needed to make a decision soon. Standing outside a hotel room in a nightgown and robe was not something she wanted to be caught doing. It was pure luck that someone had not already walked by and spotted her.

Taking a deep breath to gather her courage, Virginia turned the doorknob of the room and said a quiet thank you that it wasn't locked. She slipped into the dimly lit room, ready to do what she'd come there for.

The room was cloaked mostly in darkness. Dying embers from the previously lit fire crackled in the fireplace, preventing the room from being covered in total darkness.

"Who's there?" Charles said, sitting up in bed.

Virginia heard him fumbling around the table next to his bed. She followed the noise, drawing closer to him. "Hello, Husband."

Charles's movements stopped. "Virginia?" he questioned.

Virginia didn't reply. Her words lodged in her throat as she tried to decipher his tone. Was he upset with her for coming into his room?

A flash of light appeared as Charles struck a match. The light grew larger when he lit the oil lamp on his bedside table.

Virginia stood next to his bed looking at his features illuminated by the faint light. Her heart beat an erratic tempo in her chest. Instinct told her to run, but she refused. She held her ground, under Charles's scrutinizing gaze.

"What are you doing here, Virginia?"

Instead of replying with words, Virginia pulled the knot of her robe, opening it. Charles's eyes followed her actions. He swallowed hard, and his lips parted slightly. His gaze burned with desire. Virginia allowed the robe to fall the ground, pooling around her feet. She reached for the buttons at the front of her nightgown next.

As if being snapped out of a dream, the haze of desire cleared from Charles's eyes as he scrambled from the bed and stood in front of her. He clutched her hands at her chest in his before she could undo the second button. "What are you doing here, Virginia?" Charles asked in a serious tone.

Virginia shifted their hands so that hers were the ones holding his. She exhaled a deep breath, steeling her resolve. "I am a broken woman. I didn't realize it until I met you. You are everything I could ever need or want in a husband, and still, I pushed you away. I thought I was being smart by hiding my heart away. I lied to myself and believed that it was because I needed to dedicate my life to serving others. As if the two were mutually exclusive. But, in reality, I was afraid. Afraid to think that I was worthy of someone to love me. Afraid to love another person completely and with all my heart, because

I didn't want to put myself in a position to feel the pain of losing them. That was foolish of me. I already feel that pain of loss, by denying myself what I want."

"What are you saying?" Charles asked in a hesitant tone.

"I'm saying I love you, Charles Willcox. I want to be your wife in every way. I want to open myself up to the joy of loving and being loved by you. Even with the risk of the pain of losing you."

"Darling, I have no intention of leaving you any time soon," Charles said with a charming smile. He cupped his hands around Virginia's face, pulling her to him. His lips met hers with feather soft kisses.

Virginia wrapped her arms around his neck, crushing herself against him. She rose on her tiptoes trying to anchor herself better to deepen the kiss.

Charles chuckled against her lips. "I am trying to be a gentleman and take this slow, my feisty little wife."

"No," Virginia said in a breathy whisper. "I want our love making to be as strong and wild as our love."

"As you wish." Charles's lips crashed over Virginia's, demanding and hard. His hands bunched the thin material of her nightgown in his fists as he held her tightly against him.

Virginia moaned deep in her throat. This was it. She was giving herself over to love. Her heart still hammered in her throat, but this time with equal parts fear and excitement.

Charles slid his tongue over Virginia's lips until she opened them, granting him entrance. They tasted and explored each other until it was no longer enough. Charles picked Virginia up, not breaking their kiss, and carried her to the bed. She giggled as he threw her into the middle of it, then crawled in, stalking toward her. "Today, Wife, you become mine in every way."

"Yes. In every way." Virginia pulled Charles on top of her. Ready to make that statement a reality.

Chapter Twenty-Seven

*V*IRGINIA LAID ON HER side, propping her head on her hand as she looked down at Charles's sleeping form. She pressed the back of her free hand against her lips to stifle the smile that she could no longer seem to control. All she had to do is merely look at him, and images of how thoroughly he'd made love to her again and again last night flooded her mind. Unable to restrain herself, Virginia bent down and kissed his lips.

Charles stirred, his eyes fluttering open. "Good morning, Wife," Charles said as he looked up at her. He cuddled close and placed a kiss in the middle of her chest.

"Good morning, Husband. Did you sleep well last night?"

"Better than I have in a long time." Charles pulled Virginia into his arms and rolled so that she was on top of him. She giggled as he kissed every inch of her face and neck.

"Husband, you are igniting desires in my body I'm not sure I'm feeling up to satisfying at the moment."

"But I'm a greedy man, and you are an irresistible woman," Charles crooned as he snuggled his nose into her neck. He continued to kiss every inch of skin he could find for a few more seconds, then drew back. With one last kiss to the top of Virginia's head, he laid back into the pillows, resting his head on his forearm.

Virginia laid on top of him, her head on his chest, listening to the beat of his heart. The steady rhythm was a soothing melody. "Can I ask something of you?" she asked in a soft voice.

"Anything," Charles replied with conviction.

"Will you hold me while I read the letter from my father?"

"Of course."

Virginia rose from the bed in search of her discarded nightgown. She picked it up from the floor and pulled out the letter from her father that Charles had given her. Climbing back in bed, she cuddled close to Charles who'd sat up, his back resting against the headboard. Virginia tucked her legs under her before flipping over the letter and opening it. Charles held her at his side as she'd asked him to, gently stroking a hand up and down her arm to give comfort and support. Virginia skipped down to the section addressed to her, then began reading aloud.

My darling daughter. The fact that you are reading this tells me that you have finally opened your heart and allowed someone to love you as you deserve. Words cannot express how happy this makes me. Your mother's love is the greatest gift I have ever received in this world and I want nothing more than for you to experience that kind of joy.

I have a confession to make. I've been trying so hard as of late to find you a suitable husband because I am sick. Dying is a better description. I've fallen victim to consumption, hence my frequent coughing and the blood you've seen on my kerchief. I don't have much time left on this earth and I wanted to make sure that you were taken care of when I am gone.

Not only monetarily, but emotionally as well. Your inheritance is more than enough to take care of you for the rest of your life. But money cannot buy the warmth that spreads through your heart when you are held in the arms of someone you love.

As I write this I'm not sure if my body will last until you return from your trip, but I wanted you to know why I've done what I've done. If I do not get the chance to say this to you in person before I leave this world, know that I love you. Enjoy every adventure life has to offer. With all my love. Your father.

With trembling hands, Virginia lowered the letter to her lap. Her father was dying, and he didn't even tell her. He could possibly be gone already, and she hadn't had the chance to say goodbye. What about her chance to tell him she loved him?

That was just like him. Making decisions for her life without consulting her. Anger blossomed in her heart but was soon drowned out by guilt. It was of poor taste to be angry with the dead, and besides, no matter what, every decision he made, good or bad, came from a heart of love.

"I'm sorry, darling," Charles said with quiet empathy. "We will be on our way back to New York soon."

"Yes. Yes, we shall," Virginia said in a level tone. She turned her head to look out the window beside the bed. After all the tears she'd shed over the past several days, now she had none. Not because she wasn't upset about her father's pending demise, but because now pain held a new meaning.

She only felt it because she loved her father so much.

Burrowing into Charles's arms, Virginia sat in quiet reflection. She allowed the memories of the best moments she and her father had shared to play through her mind. The time when she was a little girl and he laid in her bed for over an hour telling and re-telling her favorite bedtime story. The time he kept watch over her, not sleeping the entire night, and constantly bathed her with a cool rag while she burned with fever.

In her anger over the friction that seemed to plague their relationship as of late, she had almost forgotten to be grateful for her father's unconditional love. "I will never forget to be grateful for your love," Virginia whispered in a voice soft with tenderness.

"Nor I, you," Charles replied, kissing the top of her head.

Virginia sat perched on the edge of the hard wooden chair in front of Mr. Chamberlain's, father's executor, large oak desk. Back rigid, hands clasped tightly around her reticule, she fought the urge to rise from the chair and run from the office. The need to be done with the entire business of her father's estate was the only thing keeping her rooted to her chair.

There was something about discussing her father's money when he had so recently passed that didn't sit well with her. It felt greedy and cold, however silly that might be. He had died mere days before they arrived back in New York. She hadn't been able to tell him goodbye, but she was happy she had the chance to give him a funeral.

She kept her eyes trained on Mr. Chamberlain, who sat in his wing-back chair, his balding head bent as he concentrated on the papers in front of him. He furiously scrawled his signature in several places before turning them to her.

"As you know," he said, his eyes glued to the papers, not looking at Virginia, "your husband signed an antenuptial contract relinquishing his common law marital rights to your property. Thus, everything your father owned is now yours. It will be held in trust, but of course, you have full rights to manage it as you see fit. Please sign at the indicated places."

Virginia took the quill he offered her and signed the papers, thus making herself owner of all her father's assets.

"Thank you," he said as she handed the papers back to him. "If there is nothing more, Mrs. Willcox."

"Actually, there is."

"And what might that be, madame?"

"I would like for you to sell my family home. Donate the proceeds in my father's name to Mrs. Ruth Washington's School for Colored Women."

Mr. Chamberlain finally looked at Virginia, his eyes wide as he stared across the desk at her. His mouth hung slightly ajar as he blinked rapidly. "You can't be serious!" he said in an incredulous tone.

"I most certainly am. Sell the home, and give the money to the school."

"As you wish," he replied with begrudging consent. His head bent again as he resumed his furious writing. No doubt he was making notes to have Virginia's mental facilities examined.

"Is that all?" Virginia asked.

"Yes, that is all," he replied, not looking up.

Never being one to overstay her welcome, Virginia rose from her chair and quickly exited the office. A smile lit up Virginia's face as she walked into the waiting area and found Charles sitting in the same chair she'd left him in. His right leg was folded over his left as he read a newspaper. "All done," Virginia beamed.

Charles looked up from his paper and flashed his charming smile at her. Virginia's heart fluttered at the sight of it. He was the love of her life, and she was grateful for that fact. He folded his paper and rose from his chair.

"Anything exciting happen?" he asked as Virginia walked to his side. He extended his arm, which she took.

"I sold my family home and donated the money to Mrs. Ruth Washington's School for Colored Women."

Charles stumbled to an abrupt halt and stared at Virginia. A slow smile spread across his face. "I'd expect nothing else from you, Wife," he said with a chuckle. "Does this mean you would like a change of scenery?"

"Yes. I think I do," Virginia replied thoughtfully.

A warm smile played on Charles's lips as we watched his wife tap her finger on her chin in thought. "And where would you like to move?"

"You know, I don't know."

"Ah, well, while you think on that, this came for you." Charles reached inside the pocket of his frock coat and pulled

THE COST OF ATONEMENT

out a letter.

Virginia took it from his hands and opened it. "It is from Alex!" she exclaimed as her eyes immediately went to the signature scrawled along the bottom of the letter.

"Then he's alive. Good to hear. Please read it aloud."

Virginia took a deep breath to calm her now overactive nerves, which made her hands shake and the letter difficult to read. Clearing her dry throat, she read aloud.

Hello my dear Virginia. I hope this letter finds you and the rest of your party well. Did everyone make it out unharmed? I will send this letter to your home in New York in hopes that it reaches you. The main purpose is simply to let you know that I am well. I have no suffered major injuries that the medic couldn't fix. The battle lasted for two days and had a death toll reached in the thousands.

The Confederates droves us back toward Pittsburgh Landing. Without the arrival of General Buell's men who knows what the outcome would have been. I am just grateful to be alive when so many of my fellow soldiers are not. The end of this war cannot come soon enough. I have seen more than enough death to last several lifetimes. Once it is all finished, I will return to my plantation and live the most mundane life possible. Again, I hope all is well with you. Until we see each other again. Alexander.

Joy spread through Virginia. Alex was alive and well. She folded the letter and tucked it in her reticule once she finished reading. New thoughts and plans swirled in her mind. The war was not over. There was still so much that needed to be done. And even once it was over, no matter who won, rebuilding would need to take place. "What do you think about moving

205

to Alabama? I want to be where we can have the greatest impact, although, in a little less participatory manner than our last adventure. I can teach, and you can practice law for anyone in need."

"As long as you are there, I'll be happy."

Virginia wrapped her arms around Charles's waist, resting her head against his chest. "Thank you for loving me so well."

"Thank you for allowing me to."